GNOME ONE LIKE YOU

A NOVEL

TOBIE CARTER

Contents

To my Yaya,

I wouldn't be here without you. Literally.

Thank you for never telling me to shut the hell up when I talked too much.

Love you, Citag!

Chapter One
Win

In certain circumstances, standing outside a bakery, staring longingly through the window at a beautiful woman could be considered romantic. Snow bathing the sky slate-gray, the lavish red and gold bows expertly placed on each lamp post, and even the metallic sound of bells jingling in the distance are the quintessential backdrop of every Hallmark movie my Nana watched when she visited for Christmas. But the heaviness currently seeping into my limbs glues my feet to the icy pavement, preventing me from walking in and whisking the woman hunched over the register to some cabin in the mountains.

"Are you gonna go in?" a surly voice grunts beside me.

I flinch, startled by the elderly lady. "Oops, sorry."

My heart skips as the woman nods to the bakery I stand outside of, trying to build up the courage to enter ever since I saw Andi behind the counter.

How long has she been back in town?

"S'cuse me." The woman dusts fat snowflakes off her musty Houndstooth jacket, pewter eyes scanning my tailored blue suit before falling to my tan wingtips. It takes me a moment to realize her slight frown is because of the tattoos showing from my open collar. "Not all of us wanna get stuck out in this blizzard."

A vibration against my leg steals my attention from the worsening storm. I pull my cell from my pocket and curse under my breath.

Solomon's name flashes across the screen, a harbinger of Christmas chaos. I peer through the window to ensure Andi hasn't seen me. Did she manage to call her brother in the short period since the woman walked inside?

"Hey, Solo."

"Where are you?" Horns blare through the speaker, a sure sign he's stuck in rush-hour traffic.

Even with the brutal lick of the Bay State wind, sweat slides down the side of my face. A quick glance at my watch shows me it's half past six, so he's nowhere near the bakery unless he got off early.

"Picking up something from…for my mom." I stumble over my words, smacking a clammy hand against my forehead.

Picking up a pie from a bakery is hardly against the law, but if Solo knew I was within twenty feet of his precious sister he'd become the old linebacker he was in high school and mow me down. Which begs the question, does he even know she's back in town for the holidays?

"You're still meeting me for happy hour at Ginger's, right?" he asks, unaware of the dilemma currently causing my heart palpitations.

Only Solomon, the perpetual bachelor, would want to go bar hopping as a snowstorm ravages Massachusetts. I take another look at the darkening sky. As a kid, being out in a storm used to be fun, a way to get into all sorts of trouble, but then Nana made me watch some of her personal injury lawyers litigate snowmobile accidents, and I haven't ridden one since.

"I dunno, man. This storm is getting worse by the minute, and I've gotta finish some work before Nana comes next week." The mention of work brings the stack of client paperwork I need to organize and the emails I've yet to answer back to the forefront of my mind.

"You don't need to get anything done." His laugh teeters on a scoff. "Nana's gonna retire and make you a partner regardless of if you have your entire portfolio wrapped in a pretty bow with her favorite bottle of Chardonnay. That class action suit you won for the firm will go down in history."

Tension inches its way up my neck at the mention of Nana's retirement. At nearly seventy, she's finally ready to relax and let someone else run the law firm she and my grandfather started and ran up until he passed in a car accident. Being their only grandson, most people would think I'm the obvious choice, but Nana's old school and wants to know I value something more than just my win-lose streak.

Not everyone deserves a sweeping love story like her and Grandpa.

"Besides, I'm sure you can find some hot chick to pose as your girlfriend when Nana comes next week." He lets out a string of curses, forcing me to pull my phone from my ear. His road rage subsides, and he continues, "The bar bunnies love a bad boy."

I poke my tongue into my cheek to prevent me from calling him out. I've worked hard the last ten years to shed the delinquent, bad boy persona I gained in high school—being the son of the Tri-State's top drug dealer didn't help—but him bringing it up still chafes. He's used to women giving me their numbers and shoving the flimsy papers scrawled with their digits into my suit pockets, but it hasn't dawned on him that I don't go home with them.

I never have.

The door behind me dings and the old lady passes me, nibbling on a cookie. "Better get in there before she closes up."

"Who's that?" Solo's voice echoes in my ear.

I peek into the window to see Andi with her dark brown hair thrown up into a messy bun wiping down counters with a candy cane in her mouth. "I've gotta run, Solo."

"Wait! Who was that? You're still meeting me, right?"

"Sure." I hang up and slide the phone into my pocket before approaching the door.

Forcing my tie back into place, I scrape a hand along my beard and go inside. Andi's grandparents' shop has been a staple in our town for at least fifty years, filled with an eclectic mix of household goods and vintage candies, its style similar to that of every Cracker Barrel waiting area.

The aroma of freshly baked snickerdoodles collides with the earthly pine of a decorated tree by the door, a familiar scent from my childhood. The multicolored lights Solomon and I haphazardly hung when we were sixteen still swoop from the ceiling, a testament to two young rabble-rousers being punished for stealing cookies. A few customers putz around, picking up little trinkets and stuffing cellophane-wrapped spice cake bundtlets into their baskets before checking out.

My favorite shelf in the corner calls to me. I sidestep a customer leaving, skirting the back wall and finding the shelf normally filled with garden gnomes of all shapes and sizes nearly empty. Andi's grandmother usually lets me know when she has a new one in stock, but it's been a few weeks since I've heard from her. Most people collect coins or comic books, but I like miniature gnomes, for reasons I refuse to explore.

My pulse quickens when I see the upside-down gnome with a blue hat, green shirt, and sunflower in its hand sitting at the front of the shelf, a new addition to the creator's collection. I'd love to learn how to make them, but I don't have the time to learn a new skill. It has nothing to do with the fact that Andi's grandmother refuses to give me the artist's contact info. I'm sure she gets a cut from selling them through her shop, so I can't fault her business decision, but as I reach for the gnome before anyone else can nab it, the righteous feeling of success wells up within me.

Andi's back is to me when I step up to the counter and set down the gnome, her shapely behind drawing my attention. It's been years since I've seen her. Gone are the gangly arms and legs I used to playfully tangle into submission over the remote, replaced by curves I shouldn't be tempted to grasp—again.

"I wondered when you'd muster up the courage to come inside." She turns around holding a box, toffee-colored eyes sharp and serious as they land on me, then the gnome. I search her face for any hint of recognition, but all I get is a slight crease above the bridge of her nose.

My mouth instantly dries, heart thumping so loudly in my ears I can't think.

It's just Andi.

I used to be able to sling barbs back and forth with this girl in my sleep. I've seen her messy morning hair, smelled her oddly sweet morning breath, the mismatched pajamas she wears to bed, even held her hair while she vomited on my shoes. So why is my chest so tight it's like I'm standing in front of a crowd giving the Presidential address?

"Winchester?" Andi's exasperated voice snaps me out of my daze.

She *knows* how much I can't stand people using my full name. I've been Win Robinson since crossing up her brother and every other guard down at the community center as kids, and I've kept that same moniker even as a litigator.

I feign a bravado I don't feel, hoping to steady the shaky ground beneath me by using her tactic. "Dandelion."

She mumbles a scathing retort I can't quite hear and plops the box down beside a newspaper opened to the rental listings section. Multiple highlighted circles draw my attention before she snatches the paper and stuffs it into her purse on the back counter.

"You came in for a...gnome?" She frowns and crosses her arms, lifting her ample bust in a way that makes it damn near impossible not to look. This woman is definitely nothing like the Dandelion I grew up with, the sweet girl who blushed every time I came into a room.

She's all fire and confidence now.

I like it.

With effort, I keep my eyes trained on her. Though it's difficult not to mention how cute it is that she's wearing a gnome shirt to fit in with the décor, I opt to answer with something less likely to have her throwing a pie in my face.

Andi loathes being called cute.

"Mom ordered one of your Grams' famous orange-anise cakes."

She drags her attention away from the gnome and thumbs through an order book, sighing heavily as if I'm the biggest inconvenience in the world. The brown skin at the corner of her eye wrinkles before her gaze lands back on me, a hot brand against the side of my face. "Let me check the cooler."

Her absence is a welcome reprieve. I didn't expect her to be so chilly toward me. If anyone has reason to be upset after this many years, it's me.

Chapter Two
Andi

Of all the people I expect to walk into the bakery, Winchester Robinson is the last person on that roster. When I offered—was volun-told—by my grandmother to come help out at her bakery, I hadn't even considered I'd run the risk of seeing him. Not that it wasn't a possibility, in the town we both grew up in, where his family's name is plastered on billboards and bus stops.

Pure lava courses through my veins that the cooler's frigid air can't soothe. I lift my shirt to feel the icy breeze on my skin, hoping it will dry my boob sweat, and cursing inwardly at the clothes I yanked on this morning as I ran out the door. Compared to him, dressed in a sleek navy suit, I look like a high schooler in skinny jeans and a gnome shirt.

You shouldn't care what he thinks about you.

Stacked boxes of cheesecakes block my view of the shelf where the order should be. It takes me longer than expected to shift them to the side and grab the cake, and by the time I return to the front, Win has managed to come around the counter and grab the newspaper I stuffed into my purse when he arrived.

"What the hell, Win," I yell, setting the box on the counter and reaching for the pages.

"Moving again so soon?" he taunts, lifting the paper out of reach. "What happened? Get kicked out of your apartment for singing off-tune? Burned the place down with your straightener?"

I cross my arms and grit my teeth, patiently waiting until he's done being an asshole. Even though years have passed since I last saw him, it's too easy to fall back into old habits of annoying each other—our old foreplay. The last thing I need is for him to go tattling to my brother—who will no doubt tell my parents—that I'm back in town. Not that they'd even care about anyone outside of their congregation, but I'd have to fess up and tell them I'm only "visiting" because I was unceremoniously evicted from my workshop.

Another thing I've failed at in their minds.

It wasn't my fault, but my parents don't need another reason to look down their noses at me, and if I have any chance of getting my holiday orders finished before Christmas, I need to make enough money to rent another shop.

"Did you need anything else, Winchester?" I sigh, feigning disinterest in the newspaper.

He places it on the counter and pulls out his wallet. His tattooed hands flex as he pulls out a wad of cash, and my skin heats as I picture the winding swirls of tattoos that snake up his tan arms and spread out onto his torso, a memory from a time long past.

He keeps them covered now, the bad boy beneath the crisp white shirt.

"Just this." He places the gnome I carved and painted on top of the cake box.

I pick it up with a pasted-on smile, my heart beating a million times a minute. Grams has been stocking my gnomes in her bakery for the past few years, but part of me worried she hid them away and gave me the money from her own pocket. After selling out the past two days, I've realized that people love my work—even if my parents think I'm a flake with no ambition.

Win clears his throat, snapping me from my daze. I should be thankful for the sale; I can't help but poke the bear.

"Your girlfriend must like *small* things."

His hazel eyes narrow, and his tongue slips out to moisten his full lips. Years ago, watching him do that would have my stomach filling with butterflies.

Apparently, nothing has changed.

"We both know that's not true." He lays his money on the counter beside the newspaper, and strides to the door, leaving me with the memory of the night I was something more than just his best friend's little sister. "Tell Grams I said thank you."

Brisk wind whips through the shop the moment he exits, taking my breath with him. I stare at the door for entirely too long, wondering how after ten years he still has the ability to make my heart flutter. I've tried to convince it that we hate him after what happened on bonfire night, but the stupid organ must have short-term memory when it comes to young love.

Ready to close, I grab the money, counting more than what the cake and gnome cost. I take the extra and stuff it into my bra; every dollar counts. I'll chalk this up to a tip for having to deal with my brother's surly best friend.

I stuff the newspaper into my purse beside my whittling set and lock the doors. Thick snowflakes fall from the gray sky. A sleek black BMW sits across the parking lot, and I struggle—and fail—not to notice the driver behind the wheel. He's on the phone, probably chatting with one of his lawyer cronies about playing golf in Mexico while I'm freezing my ass off walking to my car.

The engine sputters to life and Christmas music blares through the speakers. I'm blasted with cold air, an error on my part for not letting my brother install a remote start. I shift the car into gear, but nothing happens. A moment later the lights go out and my car dies.

I twist the key again, cringing as the engine whirs, too cold to start in this glacial air. But a few rapid clicks later it's apparent that I'll be stuck in this blizzard, and I bang my head against the steering wheel, cursing for not getting that battery jump starter Solomon sent me the link for last week.

No wonder your family thinks you can't handle yourself.

A stream of white floats into the cold car as I exhale a warm breath. I'm totaling up how much a new battery will eat into my meager savings. I'm not poor by any means—I've saved more than I've spent—but between rent for my apartment and a new workshop, things will get tight soon if I can't complete my online orders.

Hell, I'd take a garage with a saw, chisel, and a piece of sandpaper at this point.

A knock at my fogged-up window startles me. I flinch and jam my finger into the steering wheel, swearing as pain streams through my knuckles. I use my coat to wipe away the sheen covering the glass.

"What do you want?" I ask, unable to roll down the window.

Win opens the door and leans on the frame, bent down far enough I can see the flecks of green in his irises. The spicy scent of his cologne floats into my nose, and I fight the urge to inhale it like it's the last air on earth.

"Did you forget which one is the brake and which is the accelerator?" He cracks a wide smile that in another place and time would've filled my stomach with butterflies.

"You're so funny, Winchester. Did you buy that personality at the store this morning?" I sit back in my seat and huff a sigh.

"Car turn into a pumpkin, Snarkerella?"

"Something like that," I mutter.

He sighs and reaches across me to flip the ignition again—as if I wasn't smart enough to try that first—and grumbles when it makes the same clicking sound from earlier.

"I have jumper cables in my car. I'll be right back."

I heave into the headrest, silently praying that it'll work. I need to get out of here and back to Grams's house before the snow gets too bad.

"Pop the hood," Win says, holding a small jump starter—the same one Solo suggested I buy. It becomes apparent within a few minutes that Mildred, my little Corolla, is dead.

I slump forward in the seat.

Car trouble is the absolute last thing I need right now.

"Come on." Win sighs, apparently exasperated by my very presence as he holds open my car door. "I'll drive you."

He couldn't look more put out if he tried.

"I'm fine. I'll get a rideshare," I say, tapping away on my phone.

"No chance, Dandelion." He snatches the phone. "I'm not gonna let you get murdered in a snowstorm. Solo would kill me."

"Well, in that case, have fun in hell." I grab my phone back and pull up the app.

I feel his sigh before he reaches across me, steals my keys, and unbuckles my belt. His stupidly large palm hooks my side and scoops me out of the car in the sexiest maneuver known to man. Half of me wishes he'd complete the alpha trifecta by throwing me over his shoulder and giving my ass a swat, but I digress. They can't all be cinnamon rolls disguised as alphas.

Sometimes they're just plain, run-of-the-mill assholes.

"If I'm going to hell," he says, slamming my door, "You're going with me."

I cackle, and as if the universe wasn't already screwing me, I inhale the crisp air and my lungs seize, causing me to cough uncontrollably. He smirks and strolls to his car, leaving me to follow or die. Inner me wants to stomp her feet and tell him I'm not going, but the tips of my fingers are already pink, and my skin screams from the wind lashing against it.

With effort, I struggle to catch up to his six-foot-two stride, overnight bag slung over my shoulder. He's ready and waiting for me at the passenger side as if I'm a kid he needs to secure into a five-point harness.

"You really didn't have to do this," I grumble, opening the door and sliding onto the warm seats. "I can take care of myself."

"Just be a good girl and buckle up. I've got work to finish." He slams the door and walks around the back of the car. The thrill of the words 'good girl' coming out of his mouth warms my center, but his condescending tone curdles any hopes he may mean it in any other way than that I represent an inconvenience to be dealt with.

I peer into the side mirror. Win looks up at the sky, his mouth moving in a silent plea. I wonder if he's asking the Lord the same thing I am right now.

Chapter Three
Win

Crisp air burns as I inhale a large breath and force it through my nose, attempting to expel the tension that sparring with Andi always causes. The minute I wrapped my arm around her and pulled her from the car, I knew I was in trouble. Her curves fit perfectly between my forearm and biceps, and it takes everything in me to erase imagining her ample thighs resting there while I devour her.

You made a promise to Solomon to stay away. And she hates you.

I allow a moment more to freak out before I slide into the car. There was no way I was going to let someone else take her home just because she loathes me. Maybe I did it to spite her, but either way, the tightness in my chest at the image of her waiting in a cold car dissipated the moment I made the decision.

"Can you take me to Grams?" she asks, staring out the window.

The cadence of my heart matches the heavy percussive boom of "Carol of the Bells" playing on the radio, and I slowly press the accelerator. "You're not staying with your parents?"

The tires spin, then catch a hard enough patch of snow to lurch forward. Snowflakes fall, heavier now just in the short time it took to argue with her and get her in my car.

She scoffs. "I'd sooner sleep in my car."

A smile skirts my face at her admission. Her parents have always been hard asses bent on keeping up appearances and social status as the perfect pastoral family, something Andi never managed to do in their minds.

"Does Solo know you're here?" I inch out onto the main road, my fingers already aching around the wheel from the tightness of my grip. Thankfully, the street is almost empty, seeing as most people don't have a death wish and have enough common sense not to stay out as the weather worsens.

"No." She sucks in a breath. "And I'd prefer you didn't tell him I'm staying with Grams."

I frown; she and Solo used to be tight, the yin to each other's yang. He and I became best friends in middle school, though I can't quite pinpoint the moment his annoying, tag-a-long of a sister became the one person teenaged me felt most balanced around.

"Is that why you're looking for a new apartment?" I nod to the paper sticking out of her purse.

She props her arms up under her breasts in offense and my brain shifts into another dimension where she doesn't hate me and I can always touch her the way I want to. The car swerves and she scolds, "Eyes on the road, not my tits, Winchester."

I chuckle and choke on my spit, though I'm unsurprised by her bluntness. The mouth on this woman always drives me crazy. She never shies away from telling me like it is, so I'm curious why she seems so...small right now.

"I'm not looking for an apartment."

Snow clings to my windshield, and I flip the wiper to the next level, hoping it can keep up with the quickly declining weather.

"Then why are you looking for a place to rent?"

"I need a place to complete my Etsy orders," she says with a sigh. "My landlord's buddies broke a window and kept getting noise complaints but blamed it on me."

The attorney part of me perks up, already building a case against the landlord, but the last thing Andi would do is take my help. I can't blame her, not with the hurt piled between us so high it's become a wall. Ten years changes a person, but each time I look into her swirling browns, all I see is resentment.

"I fail to see how rowdy neighbors equates to you needing a new space to do...?" I have no clue what she does. After things blew up between us and I got locked up after the high school's homecoming bonfire, she was sent away. From that moment on, Solo and I had a moratorium on talking about Andi.

"He evicted me and refuses to give back my security deposit and the rent I just paid him for this month." She evades my question, but I'm sure I can figure it out with a simple internet search.

"Sounds like you've got a potential lawsuit." I slow as we come to a stop sign. The visibility deteriorates the longer we're on the road, but we're nowhere close to Andi's Grams' house.

"Says the fancy lawyer riding around in a BMW," she sighs, drawing my attention. "That requires money I don't have, that would be better spent looking for a short-term rental where I can fulfill my orders. I probably can't even afford to Uber in a luxury car like this."

I long for when I could reach over and squeeze her hand, to promise her everything will be okay. But those days are swept away like the bonfire's ashes that changed my life.

"Enough about me." She flaps wildly as if to clear the heaviness away. "How goes the world domination?"

I laugh and continue into the intersection. "World domination?"

"Your ugly mug is all over the pla—"

A honk blares and lights cut through the thick snow. I slam on my brakes and shoot my arm out to prevent Andi flying forward as a truck runs the stop sign and the car slides. We catch a patch of black ice and spin. The car whips around as I try to correct course. White knuckled, I lift my foot off the gas and turn slowly to the right. I regain control of the vehicle, my jaw clenching and my heart hammering, rage at the other driver's inattention piling up like the snow outside.

Beside me, Andi stifles a laugh. Confused and slightly worried at her weird reaction to our near death experience, I follow her gaze to where my arm—that I was using to shield her, I swear—remains in front of her, my palm directly cupping her perfect breast.

"Shit." I recoil, a bungee cord that's been snapped. "I'm sorry. I didn't...I didn't—"

"No worries." Andi's snicker fills the car.

I grasp the wheel and focus on the road instead of the pulse thumping inside my pants.

I touched Andi's breast.

Hyper aware now of the few other cars creeping along beside us, I drive slowly. Snowplows speed past on the opposite side of the road, but it's apparent the storm dumps snow faster than they can keep up. Andi is silent in the seat beside me, and I wonder what's running through her mind.

"I really am sorry." I clench and unclench my fist to expel some anxiety.

Her throat rolls with a hard swallow. She gesticulates as if batting away my comment. "It's that douchebag's fault you caught a free walk to first base."

Her playful comment about my groping settles some of my unease, and the flicker of attraction that was never quite smothered has somehow become a dull ache all over my body.

"It's really coming down." She pulls her phone from her purse. "I should probably call Grams and let her know I'm on the way."

I don't know how to respond. Sitting beside her, I'm reminded of how easy our banter used to be. Nothing was off-limits when it came to slinging insults back and forth. Stupid haircut? Check. Mom bought the wrong size pants so you were wearing highwaters? Check. Missed out on the midnight release of *Twilight* because you didn't do your chores? Check.

Being around her was as easy as breathing, but the past is a heavy weight on my shoulders, a reminder that those days are long gone.

"I don't think you've ever been this quiet," she murmurs, scrolling through something on her phone.

"Well, maybe if you'd shut up every once in a while, someone else could speak." I smile, thankful to get back on familiar ground with her. It's a knee-jerk reaction, but one that has served me well as a litigator, needing to be quick to redirect the attention.

Her sensual mouth pops open in feigned offense. "Winchester Robinson."

"Dandelion Johnson," I reply.

She growls at me and crosses her arms, struggling to spend a few minutes in total silence. Solomon's name flashes on the navigation panel, and I check my watch for the time. He's probably already at the bar, waiting for me. I glance at the passenger seat, finding Andi's pensive gaze on her brother's name.

"I can smell the wood burning over there," I say. "What's on your mind?"

"Is taking me home going to mess up your plans?"

Her question reminds me of the reason I planned on going out tonight. I'm not a stranger to having a good time and chatting up beautiful women, but it's not a beautiful woman I needed to meet tonight. I need someone willing to play my fake girlfriend. If I'm going to convince Nana that I'm the best option to take over the family business, she needs to believe I'm a family man. Or that I at least have family on the brain.

But Nana doesn't understand that I don't need to be married or have a family to be a good lawyer.

"No," I say, merging onto the highway. "I was just going to have drinks with your brother."

I leave out the part about finding a girl to pose as my long-term girlfriend. For some reason, telling Andi I've never been in an actual relationship feels like a failure. She was the only girl I'd ever considered trying with. But the minute I was vulnerable with her—when I believed whatever was forming between us before bonfire night could become real—she showed me that my past would always be a stumbling block for her.

I've never had a dad, or at least in any sense of the word. Mom tried to pick up his slack once he abandoned us, but it didn't work. I cut class to get high, got in with the bad crowd, and eventually went down the same path he did. If it wasn't for my Nana stepping up to take me under her wing when I got out of juvie, I don't know where I'd be.

I've tried to atone for my mistakes through my work as a lawyer but having a clean slate—expunged record be damned—is nearly impossible in a town where you quite literally burned bridges. Becoming a partner would prove that I still deserve to have good things in life, and I wouldn't have to work as an associate under the older partners who still look down on me.

"I doubt any bars will be open with how bad the storm is getting," she replies, then wiggles her fingers at me with a playfully arched brow. "Guess you'll have to spend time with Jill tonight."

I bust out laughing. "Only you would make a masturbation joke."

She shrugs. "Tell me I'm wrong."

"You're wrong."

It's a weird thing to feel so relaxed yet so on edge with someone. Anger, arousal, and longing swirl around in my gut as I think about what could've been between us had we not gotten in our own way. Years of therapy dealing with my dad's abandonment and my anger issues helped me see where I was at fault and how I had hurt Andi. But wishing I could change the past doesn't change the fact that I let my emotions rule my decisions and hurt the only woman I've ever loved.

She hurt you too.

Lights flash ahead of us, casting the falling snow in a muted yellow. Though there aren't many cars on the road, the red glow of brake lights unnerves me. We slow to a creep, eventually stopping in a line of cars blocked by a tow-truck. A police officer in a hooded blue parka raps on my window.

"What's going on?" Wind streams into the vehicle when I roll down the window.

"Pile-up," he says, loudly snapping a piece of gum as he slips on a pair of gloves. "Gonna have to take the detour." He points to the orange sign another officer is placing on the road.

"Okay, thanks." I nod, and he moves on to the car behind me.

"Damn it," Andi curses.

The unasked question of what happens next has already passed through my mind, but the only answer is that she'll have to come with me to my mom's house. My condo is on the other side of town, and Grams lives another ten miles away. At this rate, we're more likely to get stuck on the road and freeze to death or die from carbon monoxide poisoning than we are to arrive there safely.

My stomach clenches as the words form on the tip of my tongue. She's stubborn enough to refuse and ask me to take her back to the bakery, but I could never live with myself if I let her sleep there.

And if I'm honest, I'm enjoying being back in her presence.

I muster up my courage, my tongue heavy as it says, "We can stay at my mom's."

She toys with the string on her hoodie. "Oh, no. Just drop me off at the nearest hotel. I'll be fine."

Disappointment rolls through me, but I charge forward, unconcerned about the thin ice I'm skating on when it comes to our cracked relationship.

"Nana's coming next week so the room is set up already. Just stay the night and I'll take you home in the morning."

"Are you sure?" she asks. "I've already inconvenienced you enough."

"Dandelion," I sigh, frustrated that she can't just take me at my word. "It's eight o'clock on a Friday night during a snowstorm."

"And?"

"Last-minute reservations aren't cheap, and I don't need you to get murdered in a seedy motel so your ghost can haunt me the rest of my life."

She scoffs. "Brave of you to assume I'd spend my afterlife worrying about you."

She gnaws on her lower lip, and I inwardly groan as I remember making them red and puffy with my kisses. I recenter my thoughts with a deep inhale. I need to focus on finding a workaround to Nana's stipulation, not what I want to do to my best friend's little sister.

Chapter Four
Andi

Silence lingers after my barb until I ask, "So...how is your nana?"

A sigh leaks from the stone man beside me, causing me to frown. It didn't used to be this difficult to talk with Win. It used to be as easy as breathing. But now it feels like we're dancing around on a minefield, hoping our words don't set off any explosions.

"She's good." He changes direction as we pass the detour sign. "Finally ready to retire."

"Oh yeah?" I toy with the frayed threads on my thigh. "Isn't she like ten years past retirement age?"

His stone-faced façade cracks and a smile tugs at his cheek. "You know Nana. Still as spry in her seventies as she was in her fifties."

I nod because while I've never officially met her, I've heard enough about her from Win when we were young to feel like I know her. She's a tornado of a woman who no one would want to face in the courtroom. The sheer mention of her name and you can hear Prosecutors' knees tremble throughout the tri-state.

Already knowing the answer—it's not like I've followed his career or anything—I ask playfully, "Who's gonna run the firm when she retires?"

A moment passes, the muscle in his jaw flutters. "It hasn't been decided yet."

I scoff. "Seriously? I'd have thought you'd be the clear winner."

His face gives nothing away, but his shoulders rise with a deep inhale. "Winning cases doesn't mean everyone forgets you have a past."

A weight settles in my stomach, memories from that night barreling back into my mind.

Win borrowed his mom's car and snuck out to the junior homecoming bonfire with my brother. He was almost eighteen, and I wasn't naïve enough to think he had only come because I was there—it was a massive party—but I was hopeful. Given the way he'd worshipped my body like I was *his*, I knew there was something more between us.

It pains me to remember how much care I put into getting ready that night. I'd put on my lacy bra and thong, straightened my normally curly hair, and darkened my eyes with a charcoal pen. Operation "show my brother's best friend I'm the one for him" was in full effect.

I'd been lusting after him since my preteen years, but it wasn't until my sophomore year that he ever gave me a second glance. Sneaking kisses in the hallway when he'd come up from my brother's basement room, stealing glances across the dinner table, and fooling around in his car when he was supposed to be at math tutoring became my favorite things to do.

He was the bad boy every girl wanted, but for some reason he wanted me.

Or so I thought.

"You're the best lawyer this side of Boston," I say with conviction.

He chuckles. "High praise from you."

"Seriously, though. I'm sure your Nana knows you're the best fit for the job."

He sighs. "If only it were about my competency as a lawyer."

I wait for the explanation, but he doesn't elaborate. If we were still friends I wouldn't have to wonder what he means. I'd already know because he told me everything.

All I can muster is, "It'll all work out."

My cheeks are warm, but it has more to do with being back in Win's orbit than the heat blasting from the vents, hot enough to melt the snowflakes on the windshield. He has always been like the sun, lighting up any room he enters with his megawatt smile and effervescent charm.

A lit-up billboard stating *If you want to win your case, call WINchester Robinson,* comes into view. The sound that comes from me is somewhere between a gasp and a cackle. "Oh.my.god."

"Don't start," Win chides.

"That's *your* face," I say, mouth agape.

"Your point, Dandi?"

His gaze burns the side of my face, yet I don't look away from the larger-than-life billboard of the scowling, dark skinned heartthrob sitting beside me. I'm vaguely aware that my breath is audible in the silent car, but I can't seem to gather my thoughts.

He's too damn gorgeous for his own good.

I hate it.

Win clears his throat, snapping me out of my dream daze. Feeling uneasy about how he just witnessed me basically fawning over his billboard, like always, I find a way to even us out with a cutting remark.

"How'd they manage to smooth out all your wrinkles?"

"My wrinkles?" he replies caustically. "You know black don't crack."

I snicker and look out into the blizzard. There's no point arguing with him. He's gorgeous, and he knows it. Hell, he had the entire high school cheerleading squad throwing themselves at him daily.

No wonder his ego is the size of Texas.

We turn onto his mom's street and my heart rate ticks up when he opens the garage. The door lifts, and Win taps the brakes, halting a moment like he wonders if we're at the right house.

"Whose car is that?" I ask, pointing to a Range Rover parked in the garage beside his mom's Mercedes, blocking what I assume is Win's spot.

He pulls into the driveway and squints at the temporary plates. "No clue."

"And you're sure it's alright that I stay the night?" I've been unwanted enough—even in my own parents' home—to know when my presence is a necessary nuisance. I've seen Win's mom a few times in passing when I've come back for the holidays, and despite what happened between me and her son, she's always been so kind.

But not blaming me for her son's juvie stint and welcoming me into her home are two very different things.

He squeezes my thigh, and his touch burns me through my jeans, unfurling a long-dormant tingling in my stomach. Dark eyes land on me, hesitant in their perusal yet alight with playfulness.

"If you ask me that one more time, I'm gonna take you over my knee."

My spine straightens and my panties nearly disintegrate at his commanding tone. Who the hell am I that just his words have me considering making snow angels in a blizzard to cool off? He exits the car and comes to my side to open the door, but I'm glued to the seat.

"Don't make me throw you over my shoulder, Dandi." Win smirks as he leans in and unbuckles my seatbelt. His cologne invades my senses. "Get out. I'm cold."

"Stop calling me Dandi," I grit out, sucking in a lungful of brisk air as I brace against the snow-sleet mixture pelting my skin. Win walks ahead, pausing to inspect the Range Rover with temporary plates before he strides to the access door.

I follow, trying to keep up. Warmth from inside hits me the minute we enter, accompanied by the scent of buttered rolls and my stomach grumbles loud enough Win turns back with an arched brow.

His mom's melodic voice calls out from the kitchen. "Is that you, Win?"

"Yes." Win helps me out of my jacket, his touch featherlight yet firm. "And I've brought a guest."

"A guest?" Another voice chimes, the smoky tone familiar and I cringe at the scrape of chairs on the tile floor.

"Fuck," Win whispers. He spins around with an opened mouth as if he's about to speak when his mom and nana come into view.

"Andi Johnson." His mother opens her arms to me, her smooth brown skin flawless as always. "It's been too long since I've seen you."

"Hi, Ms. Robinson." I return the hug; thankful she holds on longer than expected. I used to look forward to her hugs. She possesses the warmth and encouragement my mom never seemed able to extend to me. "It's good to see you."

"What are you doing here, Nana?" Win asks the woman standing beside his mother.

"I came to see my daughter. I'm pretty sure that's not against the law." She pins me with a sharp look, and her brown skin crinkles at the corners with her smile as she leans on a cane for support. "And this must be your girlfriend."

I snicker, opening my mouth to say, "He wishes" but Win wraps an arm around me and replies, "Yes, this is Andi." His fingers dig into my shoulder as he pulls me to his side and pretends to kiss my cheek before whispering into my ear, "Please, just go with it."

Unable to form words, I can only manage a nod and smile at the sheer joy on Nana's face. Ms. Robinson's eyes are wide saucers beneath perfectly rounded arched eyebrows.

"We...uh...forgot the cake in the car." Win pulls me toward the garage. "We'll be right back."

"What the hell?" I yell over the howling wind as he closes the door, sleet scoring my exposed arms.

"Fuck, fuck, fuck, fuck," he chants as he lets go and paces in front of the garage. "She wasn't supposed to be here until next week."

"Win, what the hell is going on?" I demand, grabbing him to stop his dizzying stride. "Why did you just tell your Nana I'm your girlfriend!?"

I nearly choke on the words. Once upon a time I would've loved to be called Winchester Robinson's girlfriend. It was every high school girl's dream to be on the tattooed, bad boy's arm. But I learned long ago that wanting a bad boy only means you get your heart badly broken.

He massages his temples and grimaces. "I need you to do me a favor."

"I'm gonna guess it has something to do with pretending you're not the most disgusting man on the planet?"

"This is serious, Dandi." He tugs at his beard. "Nana hasn't retired yet because she doesn't think I have a life outside of my career."

"Okay, and?" I shiver and wrap my arms around my core to try and stay warm. "What does you being a loser have to do with me?"

His swallow is visible as he steps closer. "I told her I'm dating someone, and it's serious."

I laugh, surprised at the sheer look of terror on his face. "Still not following how you having a girlfriend has anything to do with me."

Win's feet become the focus of his attention. "I'm not...I'm not actually dating someone." I catch the slow rise of his shoulders as he says, "But she won't retire if she thinks I'm still single."

A lead balloon weighs down my stomach. "You want me to lie to your Nana and say we're a couple?"

"Yes," he breathes. "I'll do anything."

I cross my arms and tap my foot. "You haven't even said plea—"

"Please, I'm begging you." His palms are melded together at his chin as if he prays.

My mouth dries and everything in me wants to hail a cab or any form of transportation away from here. Hell, I'd take a small Prius complete with a nice serial killer at this point.

There's no way I can pretend to be his girlfriend. It'd be too weird, and even though it's been years and we were basically kids, we've never talked about what happened between us. I wish I could say I forgave and forgot, but the hurt still lingers. I try to cover it with snarky remarks, but there's still part of me that is stuck back at that bonfire, listening to the only man I've ever loved, laughing and calling me the worst lay of his life.

When it's apparent that I'm in shock, Win invades my space and nudges my chin up with his knuckle. "I *need* you to do this for me, please." The pleading tone of his voice makes my heart stutter. Before I can respond he adds, "I'll take on your case pro bono."

Ding. Ding. Ding.

A rush of anxiety leaves my body at those words. In the car he mentioned I have a case, but I never expected—or even thought to ask—him to represent me. I assumed with how things ended between us that I'd be the last person he'd ever want to help.

With a lawyer like Win, there's no way my sleazy landlord will get away with evicting me and refusing to give back my money. I still need to find a shop to get my orders completed, but knowing there's recourse for the grimy cretin I rented from gives me a modicum of peace.

"Okay." I exhale a harsh breath, watching the white puff dissipate in the frigid air.

"Okay?" he asks, hopeful yet reserved.

I nod. "Yeah, I'll do it if you represent my case against my landlord." I can handle one night with Nana in exchange for his help. Nothing has to change between us.

Win scoops me up into his arms and spins me around. Hyper aware of everywhere our bodies touch, butterflies flap in my stomach and I groan as he squeezes me too tight yet not tightly enough.

Surprised by the direction my thoughts have taken, I push against him. "Put me down, you buffoon."

"Buffoon?" He laughs. "That's the best you could come up with?"

"Not a lot to work with, since I already made a tiny dick comment." I shrug then smile. "That's what she said."

Win snorts. "You're something else."

Snowflakes fall on his eyelashes and my brain takes on a dream state I have to shake out of. "Okay. Let's set some ground rules so you don't fall in love with me."

He scoffs. "I can assure you that won't happen. I'm married to my career."

"Sure." I lift my hand to start listing rules.

But Win captures my wrist and pulls me close, tilting my chin up to meet his fiery gaze. "We don't need rules, Dandi. If we make this too complicated, we're gonna stumble over our stories and mess things up. I can't afford to lose my family company to someone else. So, let's make it easy. We ran into each other when you came home at Halloween, and you asked me out for drinks."

I jerk back and pretend to barf as a grin skirts his face. "In your dreams. *You* chased me until I caved and took pity on you by going on a dinner date."

"Fine, whatever." He blows air through his nose with an exasperated sigh and trudges toward the house. "We've been dating a few months but haven't told anyone because we wanted time to get to know each other again as adults."

My teeth chatter as I laugh. "You sure it wasn't because you're scared Solo will cut your balls off and feed em' to you like spaghetti and meatballs?"

He stops, and I nearly collide into his back before he spins around with a wrinkled brow. "Let's keep this between us, yeah? We just need to convince Nana we're in love while you're here and then tomorrow I'll take you home. The last thing I need is your brother thinking I have the hots for his little sister."

My shoulders fall a smidge before I correct them, hoping he doesn't notice how his words slice through me.

"Don't worry." I nudge his arm. "He knows I loathe you with a thousand suns and would probably drop a house on you if I could."

He chuckles. "Okay, Dorothy."

Chapter Five
Win

We don't need rules.

As I sit in front of Nana while Andi chats with Mom in the kitchen like they're old friends, it hits me just how bad of an idea this is. Pressure builds behind my sternum, and it's not from Nana telling me about the upcoming board meeting to discuss her retirement.

I'll have to convince Nana that Andi and I are in love while keeping my true feelings hidden from Andi.

Everyone in this small town knows how badly things ended between us years ago. It wasn't just my arrest for arson that had the high school in uproar for weeks after, but my revelation to the entire class about sleeping with Andi. For some people, an embarrassment like that could be forgotten pretty easily.

But Andi was the head cheerleader...and the local pastor's daughter.

It's my fault she was pulled out of school and sent away to live with an aunt.

"Winchester?" Nana asks, a light chuckle to her voice.

It's then I realize I've been staring at Andi for the past few minutes. "Sorry, can you repeat that?"

"How long have you and Andi been seeing each other?" She says Andi's name with a slight questioning tone, making me think she knows exactly who Andi is to me.

I shrug off my suit jacket and roll up my sleeves, baring the tattoos I cover while dealing with clients. Nana scrutinizes me, suspicious as expected, and I look back to the kitchen where my mother's laughter emanates from.

What is Andi saying to make her laugh?

"Since Halloween," I reply, moving to the roaring fireplace to eavesdrop on their conversation. "We've been doing long distance."

"And...is she *the* girl?" I don't have to look at her to know she's worried. When Nana arrived in town to pay my bail and make sure my record was expunged—not that it mattered in a small town—she made me tell her what had gotten into me, made me explain why I would go down the same route my father did. I had to tell her it wasn't drugs but a girl that sent me over the deep end, but I never told her which girl it was.

"She is," I say, as Andi and Mom burst into the room with brown boxes stacked two high. A strange swell of chivalry forces me to seize the boxes, mine and Andi's fingers brushing in the awkward transfer.

"Be careful," Nana says.

It's not directed at the women carrying the boxes, but Nana doesn't understand I don't need her warning. Therapy helped me realize it wasn't Andi's fault that I got drunk and accidentally burned down the local bridge. I can still be angry about her words, how she said to her friends we'd never work out because I was bad news like my dad, but I can't blame her for my actions thereafter. I could've easily gone home and ignored her from there on out, but I didn't.

After I got released, I wanted to reach out to her, but Solomon discovered what I said about Andi and made it clear that I wasn't to even look in her direction. In all fairness, he didn't know I was in love with her. He was used to our back-and-forth banter and assumed I still saw her as the annoying little sister, that my comment about screwing her was just a ploy to get under her skin. He didn't see the way her heart broke from my words spoken in anger in front of the entire school.

I did.

And that's the real reason I'll never have another chance with Andi.

The present iteration of which huffs at me, "You didn't have to grab those."

Feeling Nana's gaze on us, I wrap an arm around Andi's shoulder and plant a kiss atop her hair. She stiffens beneath me but relaxes quickly enough that Nana doesn't catch it. "Don't want my girl getting hurt. What is this stuff anyway?"

"Since you're here—" Mom pulls a pair of scissors from her back pocket and slides it through the tape on the box, "—you two can put up the Christmas decorations."

I groan but Andi's face lights up, her cheeks rising with a huge smile. She's always loved Christmas. I, on the other hand, rarely had a proper Christmas morning. With Dad in jail, Mom worked every holiday for overtime pay, and Nana's case load prevented her from visiting. Now, holidays are spent networking over cheap liquor or prepping for upcoming trials.

In short, the holiday season always sucks.

Nana pats my shoulder as she retreats to the kitchen with Mom whose face is alight with mischief. She loved Andi. She's always hoped we'd end up together even though I've made it clear that, given our past, that would never happen. I'm sure she's rather surprised and suspicious I've brought her home.

"I'll hang up the lights," Andi says, wielding a hammer she seems to have pulled from thin air.

I snatch it from her, ignoring her annoyed scoff. "I'll take that, Munchkin."

Through gritted teeth and a saccharine smile, she whispers, "Enough with the Wizard of Oz references, Winchester."

She whirls away and grabs a stack of bows from the box. Nana raises a curious eyebrow. Feeling the pressure of her stare, I wrap an arm around Andi's waist, ignoring the way her spine straightens, and nuzzle up to her ear. "You're the one who said you'd drop a house on me, Dandi."

A growl rumbles in her throat, but I release her and go to the basement to get a ladder. Dust particles dance in the air the moment I enter and flip on the light, sending me into a coughing fit as I descend the stairs and shuffle around antique furniture. A thick layer of sawdust covers the surface of my mom's old boyfriend's work desk, along with the tools he left behind when she kicked him out for cheating on her.

Maybe Andi can use this as a temporary workshop.

I clear it off, intent on showing Andi later, and find the ladder propped up against the drywall in the corner. Back upstairs, Andi's already tied the bows to the wrought iron bars of the staircase.

"Do you think she's buying it?" Andi whispers from the base of the ladder.

"I don't know." I sigh, untangling the lights. "We probably should've talked about PDA and how to convince her we're together. You flinch every time I touch you, and I'm sure she's going to notice if we stay away from each other."

Her chest rises with a deep breath, and she diverts her gaze as she says, "You're right. I can always pretend I'm not feeling well and just go hang out in the room, so we don't have to touch. Faking an illness around you is no problem. I already want to vomit."

"Dandelion, are you worried about me touching you?"

"No." Her voice rises in pitch.

"Are you sure? Because you've adjusted that same bow at least three times and can't even look at me when I'm talking." I reach down from the ladder and tip her chin up to meet my gaze. "Afraid you'll like it too much?"

"You wish." She smacks me away with a playful smirk. "Keep dreaming, Win."

"I do." I accidentally let the words from my brain escape.

"Wh…what?" she asks just as my phone rings in my pocket.

Ignoring her question, I climb down the ladder, answering the call without looking. My heart pounds, reminding me that it still beats for her, no matter how many times I've told it that she doesn't want us anymore.

"Dude, what the hell?" Solo says. Loud music plays in the background, nearly drowning out his voice. "Where are you?"

I plug my ear as if it'll help me hear him better. "The storm is too bad; you shouldn't even be out on the road right now. They need to close down Main Street."

"Everyone is downtown having a blizzard party," he yells over the cacophony of sound. "There's a snowball fight going on outside Ginger's Bar, you should be here!"

Andi nudges me with her foot. "Is that my brother?" she mouths before adding, "Don't tell him I'm here."

I roll my eyes in a way that conveys "duh". I focus on untangling silver hooks for the ornaments as she climbs the ladder to take over putting up the lights. "No one should be there. Go home before the storm gets too bad and you get yourself killed."

"But what about finding you a date for when Nana comes to town?" he asks.

I wrestle with my conscience on whether to tell him she's here now. I loathe lying to him, but if I tell him he'll want a full summary of what I plan to do to convince her I'm ready to settle down, and somehow, I don't believe telling him that his sister is pretending to be my girlfriend will go over well.

I like my balls attached to my body and I shudder as I remember Andi's grotesque description. I'll never be able to look at meatballs again.

"It'll be fine." As the words leave my mouth, Andi yelps and I spin in just enough time that she falls into my arms. We land with a thud on the floor, my phone clattering to the ground and sliding across the hardwood.

"Are you okay?" The pressure of her body on mine makes warmth spread through my limbs. It feels exactly right, like being in my arms is where she's supposed to be.

"Win," Solo's voice floats to my ears from across the floor.

"I'm fine." Her sweet cinnamon breath alerts me that my mom must've given her the spiked eggnog. Our gazes are entwined, bodies at just the right position that if we weren't clothed this situation would be an exact replica of many dreams I've had.

Andi scrambles off me, accidentally kneeing me in the groin. Every muscle in me tenses as pain zings between my legs and a tear forms in the corner of my eyelid. I curse when her hand lands on my crotch as if she can make the pain go away. Every nerve ending in my body lights up, and if I weren't in so much pain my cock would twitch under her accidental caress.

Realizing what she's doing, she pulls back like she just touched a hot pot.

"Sorry," she squeaks.

I wave off her concern and reach for the phone. The screen is blank when I look at it, and I can only hope he hung up before he heard her. Mom enters the room with a look of confusion on her face, Nana on her heels.

"Everything okay out here?" Mom asks, swiveling a spatula between us.

I'm still on the floor with my arm around Andi, the pain has faded and now I'm fighting for my life to keep an erection at bay. Mom takes in the wad of Christmas lights at our feet and her mouth ticks up with a smile. Nana wears a similar expression.

"We're...we're fine," Andi says breathlessly, her gaze snagged on mine. "Just got tangled up in the lights."

"Yeah, we're good." I begrudgingly release Andi. My skin hums with the imprint of her touch, and my steps are uneasy as I rise. Feeling off-kilter, I lean against the fireplace. "Dandi here just couldn't keep her hands off me."

The softest pink rises from Andi's collarbone, up her neck, and onto her face, stealing my breath. She sidles up next to me and wraps her arm around my waist, digging her fingers into my side with a huge smile on her face. "With a physique like yours, how do you expect me to do that?"

Being insanely ticklish, I jerk out of her hold, grabbing the hammer and a wad of nails to finish what we started.

"Dinner will be ready in about ten minutes." Mom backs into the kitchen with Nana whose face is lit up brighter than the Christmas tree in the corner.

My jaw clenches at the happiness on Nana's face. I know she wants the best for me, wants me to find a good woman and settle down, give her some great-grandkids. In an alternate world, I'd want to give her that too. But in reality, the only woman I've ever wanted a life like that with stands across from me with a frown on her face and no room in her heart for the likes of me.

All you have to do is tell her you're sorry.

I bat the thought away. It's not that easy; the past and present aren't parallel. I can't jump from one to the other and expect nothing to have changed. The bonfire was our point of intersection, the moment where lovers became enemies. If Andi was ever going to forgive me, it would've been years ago, but I let too much time pass, let the hurt fester too long. I'd be lying if I said there wasn't a sick part of me that is happy her landlord put her in a shitty situation where she would need my help. When else would I be able to pretend that she could be mine for real?

"Oh gosh, you're undressing me with your eyes." Andi punches me in the shoulder, snapping me from my daze. "Stop daydreaming and help me finish these decorations before they come back in here and I have to touch you again."

"You know, most women would be happy to touch me." I pin her with an arched brow as I nail the lights into the mantle.

"Most women didn't know you when you wore your mom's bonnet to sleep and t-shirts two sizes too big for you. If they did..."

"Oh, so we're going there?" I hop from the ladder after finishing the string of lights. "I distinctly remember you sleeping in said shirts every night after—"

She covers my mouth and presses up against me. "Truce."

Instinctively, I pull her closer. My body does it of its own volition, remembering a time when there wasn't any space between our connected bodies. She's only in my arms for a beat before I realize what I'm doing and release her.

"I'm sorry." I recoil with a crooked smile. "Old habits die hard."

Chapter Six
Andi

"How long are you in town for, Andi?" Ms. Robinson asks, clearing away the remnants of her delicious, deconstructed pot pie.

I grab the glass of white wine Win gives me, taking a hefty gulp before answering. "I'm here for a few weeks helping Grams with the bakery."

Although I doubt Ms. Robinson would judge me about my career choices, unlike my parents, the fear of her thinking I'm throwing my life away or that a woman belongs in an office and not a workshop keeps my tongue tied on the subject.

"You're such a good granddaughter," Nana adds, eyeing Win's arm draped along the back of my chair, slowly rubbing circles on my shoulder. It's difficult not to lean away from the touch that was once so familiar. "I'm glad my grandson found a woman who values family."

His fingers tense, and I *feel* his deep sigh. Nausea rises in my core at the sheer happiness on her face.

Happiness about a lie.

A lie that should've been our reality.

Dryness coats the inside of my mouth as I get sucked into the past. When I was sent away by my dad for tarnishing the Johnson family image, I was so angry at Win. I didn't understand why he had made those comments about us in front of everyone, why he chose to hurt me and embarrass me so badly after telling me he loved me.

It took years for me to get over it, but what I realized was that we were kids trying to act as adults. Our hormones were crazy, and the pressure to be popular was high. In my heart, I forgave him. From what Solomon told me, he regretted it the minute he said it, but the damage had been done.

If only I could let go of the fact that he never apologized, never tried to make things right between us back then. We could've moved forward together, but we're both still stuck back in that moment, allowing those hurt words to stay rooted in us.

I force a smile and lean into Win, gazing lovingly at him. "I'm glad we found each other again too."

The truth of those words clang loudly inside of me, and I wonder if he feels the same way too. Win pulls his bottom lip between his teeth, and his brown skin crinkles with a smile as he kisses my temple. "We were always going to be end game, Andi."

A knot unties in my core at the serious tone to his voice and the unmistakable longing in his gaze. Beneath the table, my leg bounces as his touch pings through my nervous system. It's not until Nana clears her voice that we break apart.

"How about some cards?" she asks with a devious glint in her gaze. "If we're gonna be snowed in together, then you guys gotta learn Three Thirteen."

My phone vibrates along the table with a text from Grams asking if I locked up the bakery and if I'm coming home for the night. I message her back that I'm staying at a friend's house. I doubt she'd tell my parents if I told her where I truly was, but I'd rather not put her in a position where she must lie for me more than she already has.

After Nana explains the Rummy-like game to us, we settle into playing and chatting about the past. I listen intently as they recount Win playing basketball down at the rec, hustling other players for their chore money before their parents would contact his mom and politely ask for it back.

"I can't help it their weak ankles made it easier for me to cross them up," he interjects as he leans close to me with a smile and says, "Dandi knows all about that too."

"There's a story there," Nana says, discarding one of her high cards.

Ms. Robinson curses her mother for messing up her set, and my face flushes as Win launches into the story.

"Solomon and I had just finished playing some video games after school and were going to take a dip in the pool when Dandi here got home from cheerleading practice." He wraps his finger around a lock of my hair and curls it, staring at me as he relives the moment. "She looked beautiful in her green and yellow outfit, and her skin was glistening from the summer heat."

I snort. "Okay, Shakespeare."

"I'm serious," he replies. "I couldn't take my eyes off you." He turns to his Nana and says, "And apparently neither could she because she was walking through the garden and tripped over a gnome statue. Scrapped her knee up pretty good and twisted her foot because she was staring at me."

His mouth morphs into the widest grin I think I've ever seen on him. I can't help the way mine follows suit, remembering the moment he's describing like it was yesterday. His shirt was off, and his abdomen rippled as he and Solo play fought. I remember thinking his dark skin was so beautiful and soft, not yet covered in the tattoos he now hides. He's right, though. My gaze followed him like there was a string attached between us. I wasn't paying attention to anything but the way his muscles flexed and the round butt in his tight swim trunks. Had it not been for that garden gnome, I could've stayed there watching him all day.

"She let me help her inside and wrap up her ankle."

I playfully push his shoulder. "I'm not sure you can call what you did wrapping, but it sufficed until my mom got home."

His gaze is the slide of a knife on a whet stone, sharp and searing when he says, "And then you kissed me."

A noise somewhere between a scoff and a guffaw scrapes up my vocal cords. "Lies. *You* kissed me before Solomon came barreling out of the house yelling your name."

He shrugs, grabs his wine, and says, "Semantics."

Heat skitters up my spine as his throat bobs with a swallow. It's not something I should notice, but it's been too long since I've been properly kissed, and even longer since I've had a man look at me like he wants to eat me for dessert. The way Win plays the part of an in-love boyfriend makes me wonder if he believes we could rebuild what burned down between us, or if he's just a good actor.

It's eerily quiet, and Win's mom and Nana smirk at each other like they're sharing an inside joke. I inhale a deep breath and pick up my cards. "Who's turn is it?"

***

Dishes clank inside the sink as I help Nana wash and dry the plates while Win and his mom ready the bedrooms. Unsurprisingly, Nana won the game by a landslide while I tried and failed to ignore the way Win's fingers traced a light pattern on my upper thigh. If I close my eyes, I can still feel the feather light touch, can imagine how it would feel on all my sensitive parts.

"Please, don't hurt him again," Nana says, her voice nearly inaudible over the gushing water.

Unsure if I heard her correctly, I say, "Pardon?"

"My grandson." Her penetrating gaze settles on me as she shuts off the water and grabs a towel. "He seems to be smitten with you."

I smile at her assessment of the situation, though I know it's not true. Is there still attraction between us? Absolutely. The man is tall, dark, and handsome. I doubt I'll ever be able to forget the way his body feels on top of mine or the way my tongue tingles just thinking about kissing him again, but outside of chemistry, there's nothing between us but the singed remnants of a fire that burned too bright too quickly and was extinguished years ago.

"He's been through a lot since being released," she continues. "And I'm not even counting what he went through before he ever got in trouble."

A thrumming sensation takes up residence in my ears, and my throat thickens with emotion. I know she's talking about Win's dad. It was common knowledge he was a drug dealer, and most people assumed that Win would follow in his footsteps. The memory of bonfire night slides into my mind. That night, my friends brought up that same argument about our relationship potential. How would my parents react to me dating a drug dealer's son? Never mind the fact that they didn't blink an eye at him being my brother's best friend. But a potential suitor for their daughter? That was too far out of the box for them to accept.

I didn't know what to say. They kept pestering me with questions I didn't have answers for, and words I didn't mean slid off my tongue, tainting the air just as Win came up behind me. The look of sheer defeat on his face still makes my heart wither.

It's not an excuse for what he did after.

My gaze floats past her to the hallway where Win and his mom pull out sheets and pillowcases from a linen closet. As if he feels me staring at him, and he looks up, winks, and blows me a kiss. I focus on Nana, giving him my back so he doesn't see the smile I'm fighting.

From the way Nana looks at me, she knows all about the reason Win made certain decisions back then. I just hope I'm playing my part well enough that she can't see through the façade we've created for her this time.

"I won't hurt him," I say, adding the *again* silently.

"I'm sure you won't, sweetheart." She pats my hand and walks toward the hallway before giving me a wry smile. "And you make sure he does right by you, too. If not, you call me."

Win passes her, and they share a few words that have him bursting with laughter. I move closer to the doorway, straining to hear their conversation as he wraps her in a hug. Grabbing the damp washcloth, I pretend to wipe down the counter when he enters the kitchen.

"Nosy much?" He sidles up behind me, and the hair on my neck rises with his closeness.

Without thought I lean back, searching out his warmth. "I have no clue what you're talking about."

He laughs, and his closeness shows me I'm not the only one seeking the comfort we've shared before. All I'd have to do is lift on tip toes and connect our mouths.

But I won't.

This isn't real.

It's a transaction, I remind myself. One where we both get exactly what we need.

His breath coasts along the shell of my ear. "So you didn't hear her tell me she hopes you're a better lover than you are a card player?"

My jaw drops, and heat creeps up my neck. I don't come from the type of family who sit around a table playing cards and spending time with each other. Dad rarely ate with us—sermon planning always took precedence—and Mom only ever wanted to talk about Solomon's sports. They never wanted to hear about the things I made in woodshop class or how I saved up enough money as a teen to purchase my first whittling set.

Win clamps down on my shoulders. "Relax. I was just kidding."

I elbow him in the side with a huff. "You're a dick."

He clutches his ribs as if I actually did some damage. "I told her you're a screamer, so she better take out her hearing aids."

"Oh. My. Gosh." Exasperated, I pinch the bridge of my nose. "I can't handle you when you're like this."

"Like what?" Recovered from his temporary pain, he leans on the counter. His Oxford is open at the collar, and the skin covered in tattoos peeking out makes my mouth water. I inhale a deep breath and put as much space between us as possible.

"When you're..." I wave at him as if that conveys what I'm trying to say.

"Handsome? Intelligent? Humorous?"

Disarming. Bothersome. Mouth-wateringly sexy. Cocky. "Annoying is the word that comes to mind."

He opens his mouth to respond just as his mom walks into the kitchen. He yanks me into him and swipes loose tendrils of hair off my shoulder. Little firecrackers shoot off in my core when he kisses the heated skin at my nape. I muffle the moan that slips out, but by the way Win stiffens, and his fingers dig into my sides, I know he caught it.

"I'm heading to bed," Ms. Robinson says, opening her arms for a hug. "I'm so glad you were able to join us tonight, Andi." Her gaze lands on Win before she says, "Your room is made up. I'll see you in the morning."

Pressure settles on my chest, making it difficult to breathe. Nana's early arrival means there's not an extra room I can sleep in alone. I knew we'd have to touch to play up the relationship in front of his mom and Nana, but somehow the fact that we have to share a room—and sleep beside one another—is too much for my brain to compute.

Win releases me and curses under his breath on an exhale. I massage my temples and try to figure out what to do. I'm silent until I hear the click of his mother's door.

"There wouldn't happen to be two beds in your room, would there?" I ask.

He strokes the side of his face, brows bunched. "It's still the same full bed I had when I was younger."

"Damn it. What about the couch?"

"It'd probably look a little suspect if Nana woke up and found us sleeping separately."

I nervously twist the hem of my shirt into a knot. We've only been in bed together once, and we weren't sleeping.

He chuckles. "I'm sure you can manage to keep your hands to yourself for one night."

He's trying to play it off, but I can tell he's nervous too by the little wrinkles that form between his eyebrows.

When I don't respond to his comment, Win says, "This doesn't have to be awkward, Dandi. We can just watch a movie or something until we're tired."

He's right. We can both be adults about sleeping in the same bed. He doesn't need to know how my heart threatens to rip through my shirt at the idea of being pressed up against him, cuddled into his massive frame.

Win could have any girl he wants. He's the best lawyer in the town, he's well educated, ambitious, and more handsome than any man has a right to be. Is it wrong to wish that I deserve him? To wish that I could go back to the night of the bonfire and shove the words that hurt him and made him feel undeserving of love back into my mouth?

I swallow against emotional shards of glass and paste on a smile. "I call dibs on picking the movie."

Chapter Seven
Win

Warmth spreads through the living room as I stoke the burning logs in the fireplace and gather my racing thoughts. Nana's words ring in my ears. My grandmother is a spitfire, a stately woman not afraid to speak her mind. When she told me she'd disown me if I let Andi get away again, I couldn't help but laugh. As if anyone could "get" Andi. I spent my younger years chasing her and my adult years chasing away every thought of her. Now that she's here in my grasp, all I want is to finally *keep* her. But once again I've fucked up and blurred the lines between us.

If I tell her how I still feel, will she think I'm just doing it because I need her to help me convince Nana?

Andi enters the room with two glasses of wine and stops by the window, peering out at the fat snowflakes dropping from the sky. A quick look at my weather app shows the storm should be stopping soon, and I turn away, hiding the disappointment at the thought of taking her home in the morning.

"Remember that winter I froze your boxers and double-dog-dared you to go make snow angels?" Andi chuckles, sipping her white wine as she extends a glass to me and settles on the couch.

"I doubt I could forget something that brutal." I place the poker in its holder and grab the remote, throwing it to her on the couch. Watching a movie until we're both tired was much more for my benefit than hers—I'm too riled up to sleep next to her without touching her. Instead of sitting beside her, I opt to throw a pillow on the ground and relax against the cushion. "I'm pretty sure my cock still doesn't work right because of the frostbite."

She leans forward and flashes a devious smile. "They make pills for that, you know."

The sweet smell of her breath stirs my stomach and seizes my lungs. I look over my shoulder to return a snarky comment but she moistens her lips and all I can think about is what it would feel like to kiss her again.

Kisses with Andi were never the typical awkward teenage kisses where you try to eat each other's faces. Her mouth was always soft and searching, pliable yet firm, and I could never get enough of the way her tongue moved against mine or the noises she'd make when I'd deepen the kiss.

My cock involuntarily jumps at the thought of exploring whether or not she still makes those noises and if there are others I can draw from her.

"What do you wanna watch?" I ask, changing the subject before I get blue balls from memories.

"The TV would be my first choice, but someone won't stop talking long enough for me to figure out this remote." She jabs me in the shoulder with her foot. I grab it and press my finger in the spot I remember she's ticklish, but her scowl is playful as she jerks away. "How the hell do you work this thing? It has like twenty buttons on it and that's not including the little dials on the sides."

"It's a universal remote, Dandi. Just press the power button then the button for Netflix."

"Got it." She sucks her teeth and focuses on choosing a show. "What about a Christmas movie?"

I shrug, staring at the column of her neck and wishing I could feel if her heart is racing as fast as mine. "Sure, Die Hard should be on Netflix."

She scoffs. "Die Hard is not a Christmas movie."

"Dandi." I feign disbelief, splaying my hand across my chest. "It absolutely is, and that's a hill I'll die on."

Her laugh fills my stomach with giddy, excited butterflies. "Then I guess I know where to bring flowers to your grave."

Happy to be back in her presence with our easy banter, I ignore her jest. Unsurprisingly, she chooses one of those craft competition shows she loved to watch after school before her parents got home. We fall into companionable silence, but I don't miss the little comments she makes about each contestant's woodworking prowess, which reminds me of the deal we made.

If I'm going to represent her, I might as well do my research.

"How long did you lease your woodworking shop for?"

She inhales a large breath before answering. "For a year."

"What types of things do you produce? Furniture? Décor?" I can't picture her working over a wooden sign that says "Live, Laugh, Love". She hasn't commented on any singular piece of furniture she's encountered in my mom's house, and believe me, there are plenty of antique items in every dusty corner.

She catches her bottom lip between her teeth, and I inwardly groan. "Don't laugh. I know it's just a stupid hobby."

"I wouldn't dare." I give her the boy scout's honor.

Anxiety curves her posture as she wraps her arms around her legs.

"I make those little gnomes...like the one you bought today."

My eyebrows lift. "Really?"

She sheepishly nods. "Yeah. I guess...ever since that day I've had a fascination with them."

I fail to conceal the smile that wants to burst free. What are the odds that a singular moment made such an impact on our lives that we both found a love for the same thing?

I glide my thumb across her knuckles. "I have pretty much every gnome your Grams stocked in the bakery. I never knew it was you that made them though."

"No, you don't." She waves me off, probably assuming I'm just placating her.

"Look at me," I beg. Her shining browns land on me, and my chest crowds with too many emotions. Whoever made her feel like her work didn't matter is number one on my shit list. "If you saw my office desk, you'd probably think I'm crazy because of how many little gnomes I have. They call me 'Sherlock Gnomes' at work."

She bursts out laughing, and the apples of her cheeks pinken. Relief floods my body as she relaxes into the seat, wiping happy tears away. "You're lying."

"Gnome I'm not." I crack a wide grin. "Do you know how often the guys at work come up with gnome puns to antagonize me? It's become somewhat of a running joke."

"I'm sorry," she says with a smile that conveys there's not an ounce of remorse in her body.

"I'm sure you are, but that's beside the point." I nudge her knee with my elbow. "I don't ever want to hear you call something you're passionate about a 'stupid hobby' again. Understand me?"

She looks off to the side, refusing eye contact. "Sure."

"I'm serious, Andi. You. Are. Talented." I softly grab her chin, guiding her to look at me. "Most people don't have a creative bone in their body, but your work speaks for itself. You're obviously good enough that people pay you to make them through your Etsy shop and buy them at the bakery. Whoever made you feel like your work isn't important is an idiot. And we don't listen to idiots, do we?"

A blush moves down to her collarbone, and it's entirely too difficult not to follow the movement with my finger. She finally nods, and I feel like we can return to the conversation.

"So, what's been going on with this landlord?"

She crosses her arms, and a slight frown mars her face. "I was six months into the lease before things started…happening."

My nostrils flare, and I grit my teeth as I cycle through all the things that could be going wrong. "What's been *happening*?"

She fulls a face that's somewhere between a glower and a pout she gets comfortable behind me, her feet resting along my upper back. "These juvie kids started hanging around his house, coming and going at all hours of the night."

"How do you know they're juvie kids?" Tension inches up my spine. I was one of those kids, a product of bad circumstances that didn't make good decisions but still turned their life around.

"A probation officer drops them off weekly after their drug test. They're just troublemakers." She must sense my discomfort because she squeezes my arm and says, "I'm sorry."

"You have nothing to be sorry for," I reply, wrapping my pinky around hers the way we used to do beneath the dinner table. "I made my own decisions."

Being this close to her, it's easy to slip into the memory of the night that changed our lives. I wanted to go on a midnight stroll to look at the stars so I could ask Andi to officially be my girlfriend, but when I found her huddled with her friends, talking about me, I couldn't help but listen more closely. What I heard set fire to my self-esteem and what could've been our future.

Andi connects the rest of our fingers, snapping me from the momentary daze. Her palm is warm against mine, and a weight lifts from my lungs at how natural it feels between us.

"My words are what caused you to make those decisions, and for that, I am sorry." She sniffles, and tears brim her lashes. My breath quickens, squeezing my lungs in a vise. I wasn't prepared to hash out the things that severed our connection, but if we're ever going to move past it, it must be now.

I swipe away a falling tear and she continues. "I didn't know what to say when my friends kept pushing, and instead of telling them how amazing you are, I let them think that you weren't good enough for me...I made *you* think you weren't good enough. I'll never forgive myself for that."

A solid lump of emotion blocks my reply from coming out. I allow the fire burning through my veins to scorch every bit of pain or anger I held towards her for too long.

"Thank you." I kiss her palm. She doesn't blanch away, keeping our fingers interlocked. "I needed to hear that."

It's the truth. For ten years I've carried around this idea that I wasn't good enough and didn't deserve good things because of her words. Not because I was upset with her for saying them, but because I believed they were true. Most people expected me to fuck up, to be exactly like my father. Andi was one of the only people who saw me for me, so when I heard her words it was like an umbrella collapsed and let the assumptions of everyone else rain down on me too.

"And I'm sorry, too. I never should've said those disgusting things about you."

She shrugs. "It's okay."

"No." My voice strains. "If we're talking about the past, I want a clean slate going forward. I was hurt when I heard you talking, and I wanted to hurt you too. I didn't think about how it would get back to your parents or what they'd do when they found out we'd been together. It was my fault you were sent away to live with your aunt."

She stops me with a finger on my lips. "Living with my aunt was a thousand times better than being stuck under my parents' roof with their prized child."

The downward curve of her mouth sets my teeth on edge. I love her brother. He was the first friend I made when we moved to Massachusetts, and he's been my best friend ever since. But I know how much his parents favored him over Andi. His sports, his academics, his everything, came above anything Andi needed. They always made Andi feel like a second-rate citizen in her own house, made to earn their love by accomplishing things and following the rules.

"It still doesn't change the fact that I hurt you, and I hope you can forgive me."

She nods, acceptance of my apology clear in her smile. I inhale and exhale a deep, cleansing breath, thankful the slate is finally wiped clean.

"So, back to your landlord. He had some kids hanging around and what happened?"

She stares at me for a beat before launching into a list of everything her landlord's done from paying teens under the table for work to her finding the door unlocked and the heat turned down after he yelled at her about the electricity. Anger boils beneath my skin when she tells me she used the money she saved for a vacation to the Bahamas to replace a window after someone broke in and stole her table saw and some other expensive tools. Her case is solid, and I have no doubt I'll be able to win it for her.

"But yeah, that's why I came back and am working with Grams. I need the money to find another place, or at least rent time at a workshop to get my orders done before Christmas."

My mind floats back to the workshop in the basement. "I'd have to clear it with my mom, but there's a workbench and tools in the basement I'm sure you could use...if you want."

Her eyes light up. "Really?"

I nod. "The tools have just been sitting in there getting rusty."

She drags me into a hug, and her warm body pressed against me draws a groan. I collapse into her embrace, allowing the years of tension to melt away. I wish this was the beginning of something more than just our friendship rekindling, but I'll take whatever she's offering.

"Thank you so much, Win." She excitedly waves, accidentally knocking over her wine glass. We both reach for it, her securing the bowl while I snag the stem. The glass weeble-wobbles, splashing wine down my shirt before righting itself on the table.

"I'm so sorry." She grabs tissues from the end table and presses them against my shirt. Her eyebrows are drawn together, a look of concentration on her face. This close, all the fractals of browns and greens that mix to make up her eye color shimmer in the light from the fire.

I stop her fretting, right above my thundering heart. My skin thrums from her touch, and our closeness renders me tongue-tied and light-headed. Saliva fills my mouth as I draw her near, begging to erase the distance between us.

"Win..." Her voice is a breathy moan that pours lust into my veins. All inhibition flies out the window when she closes the distance and connects our mouths. We walk a fine line, exploring the curves of each other's mouths, familiar yet new. Goosebumps break out along my skin when she drags her tongue across the seam of my mouth, asking for access. Minutes pass in a blur as we taste each other, our teeth clinking with the ferocity of our kiss.

My cock roars to life, painfully hard against the too tight dress pants I've yet to change out of since arriving home. With a tug, Andi slides into my waiting lap, and I position her at just the right angle to reconnect us. Having her in my arms is like I've stolen a little piece of Heaven, where all the good people get what they deserve.

"Fuck." I drag out the word as I exhale, nipping along her jaw. Her lips are puffy, and her cheeks are pink from my beard brushing against her smooth skin. My fingers dig into her hip bones, begging her to stop moving yet crying out for her to move faster. All those old feelings barrel back in like a boulder, knocking down every mental block I had when it comes to my best friend's sister.

Solomon could be standing here right now, and I don't think I could stop. Somewhere in the back of my mind, I wonder if this is all part of the ruse, a facet of the part she's been playing all night to convince Nana that we're together.

Nana isn't around, though.

I bat the negative thoughts away and pour every ounce of my soul into kissing her back. If this is the only time I'm allowed to touch her like this, I want to burn this memory into her mind. My brain empties of every thought except for the feel of her mouth and the taste of her tongue. Feverish heat spreads throughout my body, a fire coursing through my veins eating up every reason I should stop this before it goes too far.

She's my best friend's sister.

She broke my heart.

I broke hers.

She's only playing a part.

None of that matters as I release her messy bun and tangle my fingers in her curly hair. It fans out down her back, and the fire casts a glow around her chestnut strands like she's an angel. Why God would send an angel like her to a sinner like me is a mystery I don't want to solve.

Must've been a clerical error.

Making out with Andi in my childhood home would seem lame to most, but it's a dream come true to me. She's always been a passionate kisser, demanding and vocal about the things she likes. She nips my bottom lip, drawing a growl from me as her body moves against my erection, and I nearly strip her bare on the living room carpet.

"Andi." I barely manage to get her name out past the lust clogging my lungs. There are things I want to talk about before we cross a line, but my body isn't accepting signals from my brain. When I don't continue with my statement, her invasion of my senses restarts, pressing soft kisses along my jaw. I'm sure her skin is aflame from my beard, but apparently, she doesn't care.

I wonder how she'd feel about beard burn along her inner thighs.

A cleared throat behind me douses the flames dancing between us. Quicker than I thought possible, Andi's off my lap and back on the couch.

"Might want to take that back to the room," Mom says, a slight smirk on her face. "Don't need Nana having a heart attack."

Coughing out a laugh, I look at Andi whose gaze is now shuttered as if she's already regretting what just happened. Disgust slides down my back. Did I take it too far? One kiss doesn't mean she wants more, but I was the one who pulled her into my lap and trapped her there.

I open my mouth to apologize as Andi stands and says, "We should probably get to bed."

Chapter Eight
Win

My feet are cinder blocks as I lead Andi to my childhood bedroom, desperately hoping I haven't ruined the progress we made tonight. Inside, the walls are still gray with black accents and leftover posters from my pop-punk phase. Back at my house, paintings from my favorite artist, Jameson Brooks, hang in every room, a testament to how I've grown from a troubled rabble-rouser to a dependable grown-up. Haphazardly placed in the middle is a full mattress with a wooden frame my mom's ex-boyfriend made in the workshop downstairs. Perspiration is a second skin as I stare at the bed, worried about its integrity knowing the half-assed job he did of loving my mom.

"Do you mind if I take a shower?" Andi asks, rubbing goose-bump covered arms. I nod and grab some clothes from my dresser for her to wear. "I can just grab my bag from the car."

"No way, munchkin," I say, trying to lighten the mood. "There's a blizzard out there and the car is already covered. Here's a pair of sweats, a T-shirt, and some boxers."

She playfully scowls at me. My heart stutters, thankful the awkward tension from before has dissipated some.

"Thanks, but I'm not wearing your underwear," she says, her tone matter-of-fact, crossing her arms in front of her breasts.

I notice the peaked nipples she's trying—and failing—to cover and bite down on my lip. Let's see how far she's willing to take this.

"The other option—" I waggle my brows at her, "—is going commando. I'm fine with that, too."

Her hazel eyes widen to saucers. If she wore pearls, I'm sure she'd clutch them, and I bite my tongue at my mistake. "Sorry," I say, "that was inappropriate. I'll get out of your hair."

Her soft voice stops me as I hit the doorway.

"What did you say?" I ask.

She blows a raspberry, and her shoulders rise with an inhale. A tendril of hair falls, caressing the side of her face before she tucks it behind her ear and looks up at me with a small smile. "Thanks," she repeats, fiddling with a thread on her pants. "For everything."

It takes everything in me to stay planted where I'm at instead of walking back and stopping her fidgeting. I hate how unsure she is, how she feels so indebted to people for things that should be freely given.

"Anything for you," I reply truthfully and leave before I say something stupid.

It's may have been years since I spent any length of time around Andi, but I'm hoping she still likes a cup of tea before bed. I quickly run out to my car, nearly giving myself frostbite as I grab Andi's overnight bag. I lay her bag at the bathroom door and escape to the kitchen. The whir of the microwave alerts me to my mom's presence as I approach. I stop outside the entryway to gather my thoughts, smoothing down my rumpled dress shirt, courtesy of Andi's roaming hands.

"I heard your sigh halfway down the hall, son." I stall my stride and pull my shoulders back, feigning a nonchalantness I hope conveys everything is normal.

"I didn't sigh," I reply, reaching into the cupboard for two cups.

Mom tsks me, clinking her spoon along the side of her cup before placing it down on a folded napkin. Her gaze burns the side of my face as she brings the cup to her mouth. Only my mother would drink coffee at nine o'clock in the evening and go to bed. I'm half convinced that means she's a serial killer, but I've yet to prove that theory.

"Trouble in paradise already?" she asks, leaning against the counter. "Seemed like everything was going well earlier."

I cringe, and heat burns my ears. No one wants to be caught by their parents getting hot and heavy. Add in the fact that we're lying and putting on a show—that feels more real than I care to admit—and it's even more embarrassing.

"No," I reply. "Everything's fine."

She stares like she's waiting for me to elaborate. When I don't, she asks, "How long do you plan on keeping this up?"

"What do you mean?"

Her gaze narrows, and she arches her tweezed brow in the way only a mom who knows her son is lying would. A chill skitters down my spine.

She knows. Of course she would. She's the most intuitive person I've ever met, yet she somehow can't tell a piece of trash boyfriend from a good man. I hope Nana was so happy I brought someone home that she didn't really look deeper.

Figuring it's best not to keep lying, I say, "Would you believe me if I said the rest of my life?"

Her slight chuckle eases the tension in my neck. "What are you doing, son?"

I grit my teeth and flex my fingers at my side. She's asking questions I don't have answers to, and I desperately wish I knew what I was doing in this situation. When I offered Andi a ride home, I never imagined we'd end up in this fake relationship. But I can't deny the thrill that shot through me when we found ourselves in this predicament, one where I could have a slice of the future I once thought would be mine.

Nana wanted to know I value something other than my career, that I could have a life outside of working for the firm, but the reality is that the only life I ever wanted was one where I came home to the woman currently in my shower.

"I don't know." I shake my head and inhale the hazelnut coffee wafting my way. "Tonight wasn't supposed to go like this."

"Like what?"

I tear off the tops of two tea bags and place them in the cups while the electric kettle boils. "Nana wasn't supposed to be here yet. I thought I had time to find someone..." I pause, face flushing in embarrassment. "Someone to pretend to love me."

"Oh, Win." She reaches for me, but I can't look at her. "I don't think there's any pretending going on here. That little scene earlier in front of the fireplace didn't look like pretend."

My shoulders drop, jaw flexing as I divulge my deceit.

"I promised her I'd take a case against her landlord pro bono if she pretended to be my long-term girlfriend. What you see is her playing a part."

Mom knocks on the counter, drawing my attention. "That girl isn't playing a part. She's had stars in her eyes since the day she met you. And those same stars burned a lot brighter tonight."

I think back on the evening. Putting up decorations, Andi falling into my arms, dinner and cards with Nana, the kiss in front of the fire. Was it all just for show? Or is my mom right in saying that Andi still holds a flame for me?

"I wish that were true." The pop of the kettle ends our conversation. I pour the hot water into our cups and scurry to the door.

"Winchester." Her stern tone glues my feet to the floor. "If you still love her like I think you do, you need to be honest with her. Don't let more time pass when you've already lost so much."

Unable to force words through my thick skull, I nod and keep walking.

"And be honest with your grandmother or she'll beat you with her cane when she finds out." Mom's chuckle follows down the hallway.

Back at my door, I take a moment to recenter before going inside. It's quiet, and I can tell the water isn't running any longer. Andi must be in bed already. I stare at the cups of tea, cursing myself for crossing a line earlier. We were on good footing before the kiss, and the agreement between us was crystal clear. Now, everything is murky, and I can't see if I'm about to step on a solid rock or get bitten by a snake lurking beneath the water.

A gust of air leaves my lungs when I find Andi inside my bed.

Dark hair cascades down her shoulders, wet and wavy. Her skin glistens, face clear of the minimal makeup she normally wears, and the white t-shirt I gave her fits tight around her bust line and loose everywhere else. She had her clothes, yet still chose to wear mine.

It doesn't mean anything, Winchester.

But it's not those things that send my pulse careening over the hill. It's the smile she gives me, the one that lights up her entire face and makes my stomach flip.

"Is that tea for me?" She scootches back and the cover falls from her legs, revealing smooth thick thighs that make my mouth water. She doesn't wear the sweats I gave her, and if my cock wasn't already awake, it is now.

My thoughts scatter, and heat rushes straight to my groin. There's no way I'm going to be able to sleep beside her all night. My fingertips twitch with the memory of how soft her skin was, warm and supple breasts peaked and ready for me, the way her full hips fit perfectly into my waiting hands.

She's perfect.

She's mine.

Only because she needs your expertise, my masochistic mind reminds me. Sure, this whole faking dating thing started as a way to convince Nana that I was serious about the future with someone, but that was back when I assumed I'd be playing the part opposite someone I didn't actually care about. Someone I could never see spending my life with.

Back before it was Andi who stepped up when circumstances threw her back into my orbit.

Minutes pass as I stare at her, and I resign myself to the following facts: My heart still belongs to Dandelion Johnson—it always has and always will, and I have exactly one night to prove it to her.

Chapter Nine
Andi

Arousal is a tangible, thick presence creeping up my skin. Win leans on the door jamb with two cups of tea, steam rising from the rims. His heated gaze hungrily traces every curve of my body, and when his tongue darts out and swipes along his bottom lip, I swear I feel that lick between my legs.

"You still like a cup of tea before bed, right?" His voice is husky, like he's finding it just as hard as I am to find breath in this small room.

I nod, clamping down on a smile. "I can't believe you remember that."

And that you braved a blizzard just to get me clean underwear.

He chuckles and sets the cup on the nightstand. "I remember everything about you," he replies in a soft voice with a weak smile, turning away from me. He stops at the dresser and pulls out clothes for himself, and I rub at the ache in my neck, wishing I could formulate the words inside my brain.

It's easy to believe when we're alone and there's no one to act for that this is all real. But Win has always been a smooth talker with keys to unlock the hidden desires in my heart.

I suck in a breath as I'm pelted with a vision of how things could've—should've—been had I not let others' opinions of my life choices mean more to me than the man I wanted to share that life with.

The house with the white picket fence was always our dream.

Lying on top of Win's old Corolla, we'd pretend we were building a two-story house complete with four bedrooms and two-and-a-half baths, a loft for the kids' toys and games, a garage for the muscle cars Win always wanted, and a wraparound porch with a swing where I could have my nightly tea and listen to the mockingbirds during mating season.

It was the perfect house. One we promised to fill with all the love that we never received from our parents. Win knew I was the black sheep of my family—my parents only valued the male heir and felt I should be the homely wife doting over my husband, not working—and I knew he wanted to make an honest living, unlike his jailbird father.

"I'm gonna shower," he says almost to himself before heading into the bathroom.

My gut twists, filling with concern. He's unable to look at me for longer than five seconds. Just twenty minutes ago his tongue was so far down my throat he was basically Venom taking over my body. I don't want to mess things up or ruin the progress we've made tonight, but there was a spark.

Or at least I thought there was.

I slide my fingers through my hair, pulling at the strands in frustration. Maybe Win is looking for some no strings attached fun instead of something long term. Had Nana came next week, he would've had someone else playing the part I am now, and who knows what that would've entailed.

I grip the blanket, annoyed with my own thoughts. I decide it's not a big deal if he wants a no strings attached night. I can do casual...I hope. I haven't been with anyone in longer than I care to admit, but the chemistry between us has been smoldering for years.

And I want to explore it.

The splash of water against the shower tile motivates me to throw off the covers and slide out of Win's bed. Grabbing the sweatpants he let me borrow—though he knows I get too hot at night to wear pants—I pad to the kitchen, searching for the gingerbread flavored whipped cream Win's mom put into my drink earlier. After securing it, I stop in the living room and grab a few decorations from the box we rifled through before dinner. I'm back in the room, curled under the covers with my tea and the decorations shoved under the bed when a freshly showered Win saunters into the room.

Beads of water glisten on his inked dark skin, rolling over firm pecs with pierced nipples and a ripped abdomen that converges into the sharpest V I've ever seen. The way my jaw drops is comical, a mirror image of how my heart slides into my stomach with a heavy thunk. His toned biceps and massive traps flex as he hangs his towel on the back of his closet, and it takes more self-control than I expect not to show him how affected I am by that image.

The Winchester in front of me is not the tattooed bad boy from my youth, the one who made me swoon and stole kisses in the hallway of my parents' house.

This Winchester is pure sin, no longer interested in making me swoon but on a mission to make me *scream*.

I somehow manage to stop drooling and drink my tea, savoring the notes of cinnamon and nutmeg mixing with honey and clove as Win grabs his cup and comes to bed. Tea shoots up my nose when my gaze lands on a decidedly not small dick outline on his sweatpants.

He flashes me a smug smile. "You okay?"

He knows exactly what he's doing, walking around without a shirt, showcasing piercings I'd love to lick and wearing gray sweatpants that leave nothing to the imagination.

"I'm fine," I croak, nearly jolting from my spot when he touches my face.

I wait for him to remove his hand, but his thumb traces the curve of my mouth. Once. Twice.

"You have the most perfect lips," he says on a sigh.

Glancing up at him, I watch his eyelashes flutter and feel his minty exhale before he releases me. Heat pours into my veins, and my arousal becomes a living, breathing monster.

Surely, he wouldn't be touching me—saying things that make my heart flutter—if he wasn't interested in seeing where this could go...right?

He leans past me and flicks off the light, depriving me of the beautiful image that is his toned upper body. "I'm sorry for kissing you earlier. I shouldn't have done that. Goodnight."

Or not.

Angry wasps swoop in and kill the butterflies that were flapping around my stomach moments ago. With my parents and brother, I struggle to stand up for myself, for the things I want in life. But I never had that trouble with Win. I was never scared to tell him my darkest secrets and desires, or to bare my soul to him and know that he wouldn't think I'm silly or a waste of space.

I nervously smooth the cover, toying with a frayed edge. So much has changed since those days, and I'm worried my forwardness will scare him off. Or worse, that he truly isn't interested in revisiting what we once had.

Stop doubting yourself. You know what he felt.

The covers rustle as he slides beneath them, resting on his side, his dark skin illuminated by the moonlight streaming through the window. I gather a steely breath as I muster the courage to call him out on his bullshit. The room is quiet except for a gurgling humidifier and my thundering pulse. I push away every instinct saying I'll be rejected and squeeze his taut obliques to get his attention.

"I kissed you, not the other way around," I say before playfully adding, "One of us had to grow some balls."

He sucks air through his teeth, twitching as my fingernails dance lightly along his side. Falling onto his back, he faces me with a wicked smile. "Got my balls on your mind tonight, Dandelion?"

I scowl, wishing he would stop playing around and be serious for once. My skin prickles when he inches closer and caresses my thigh. I inhale as one-by-one my nerve endings light up. What feels like a minute passes as Win toys with me, tracing circles on my bare hip, just east of where I'm throbbing.

"What is this?" I ask, breathlessly.

"This?" His voice is curious, but his fingers are confident as they glide up beneath my shirt, resting on my hipbone as his thumb grazes my stomach. "What do you want it to be?"

I fight the urge to roll away from him. A direct answer is what I'd like, but anxiety slides back into my mind. If I tell him I want us to try again, will he be immediately turned off by the potential commitment? Or should I keep it light and see where it goes?

The latter wins out, and I say, "One night. No strings."

A breath rushes out of him as he stares at me, dark eyes swirling with desire. Hesitation is written all over his creased forehead a moment before he closes the distance between us and captures my lips in a bruising kiss. He draws me flush with him, parting my legs with his knee. The dick print on his sweatpants pales in comparison to the weight pressing against my thigh.

Warmth swells beneath my ribcage, lapping against the dam of emotions I've built to protect my heart from breaking the way it did the last time. Overtaken by the sensation of our tongues and teeth clashing, we battle for dominance as we careen over the hill of desire. I pull away, panting as I try to catch my breath. Win takes the opportunity to flip us and secure my wrists against the mattress.

I wiggle beneath him, clamping my thighs so he doesn't see how soaked I am for him. There's something about being restrained that gets me going in a way I'm not ready to inspect.

Win's gaze lights my skin on fire as he catalogues my face then settles on the space where his cock nestles between my legs. Its heavy presence on my clit taunts me, spurring me to rock, begging for more pressure. He licks his full lips—an act that makes my pussy clench—and secures my wrists above me. The weight of him lifts off me, drawing a whine.

"What are you doing?" I whine like a petulant toddler.

"Look at me, Andi." His gravelly voice scrapes along my neck, turning my stomach into putty. I hold my breath as I face him. "Are you sure about this?"

I snort. Am I sure about this? No. Not in the slightest. The last time we did this, it had real life ramifications, ones that left scars so deep I'm sure they're imprinted on our souls.

But that's not what he wants to hear. His hold on my wrists trembles, and his eyes hold a mixture of hope and fear. It's him that's unsure. Is he worried things will go south again and have lasting consequences neither of us are prepared to deal with? Or does he know—like I do—that one night could never be enough to quench the never-ending thirst for each other?

A slow smile builds on my face and I tilt my hips, signifying I want this. "About as sure as I am that you shouldn't have gotten that ugly haircut in eighth grade."

He chuckles, forehead resting against mine for a moment before he kisses me softly and says into my ear, "I missed that smart mouth of yours."

A moan eeks out of me at his husky voice. Adrenaline spreads through my veins making me hot with anticipation as I wiggle out of his hold. He stands so I can release his erection, and the hair on the back of my neck rises as I stare down the Burj Khalifa of dicks.

He nudges my chin up, a wicked smile on his face. "Cock got your tongue, Dandi?"

"What the hell, Win." I laugh entirely too loud then cringe, hoping I didn't wake up his mom and Nana.

Heat flickers to life inside my stomach, and I yelp as Win's toned biceps wrap around my thighs and slide me down the bed with such force the fitted sheet pops off the mattress.

"What are you doing?" I squeak.

One side of his mouth quirks up, and the way his tongue slides out over his lips almost suggestively, is pure torture. "I've been waiting ten years to taste this pussy again." A corkscrew of lightning shoots through me, and my core throbs. Win pulls my lace panties to the side and leans forward, soaking his beard in slickness. "And I'm not waiting a second longer."

His words send a shiver down my spine. He stares at me for what feels like hours, taunting me, then with a wicked grin goes to work, lapping me like hot butter. Sparks shoot off in my core as I writhe beneath him, and a deep groan rumbles from his chest. A slow lick at my clit builds pressure in my core. Beneath my cotton t-shirt, I palm my heavy breasts, rolling my nipples between two fingers.

Cool air hits my core as Win retreats. "Andi," he husks.

I groan, pushing my bottom toward him, begging for his touch. "What?"

"Stop touching yourself."

The independent woman in me wants to snap back at him like I always do—push when he pulls—but the deep tone of his commanding voice makes my inner walls clench as if it can keep my arousal at his domineering a secret. It's in my nature to challenge him, but this time I don't.

Slightly irritated, I release my sensitive nipples with a sigh.

"Good girl." He swats my pussy, and I arch off the bed.

"What the hell was that?" *And why did I like it so much?*

He chuckles. "Just teaching you a lesson."

I press my heels against his back, beckoning him closer to my core. He might think he's got the upper hand, but it'll be me that brings him to his knees.

"Stick to litigating. You're a shitty teacher."

Breath whooshes out of me when he presses his thumb to my throbbing clit, drawing small circles that make me dig my heels into the mattress. The ripping sound of my lace panties seems to echo in the silent room, and somehow Win manages to not detach himself from me as he deposits them at the foot of the bed.

His sensual mouth closes around the apex of my thighs, drawing moan after moan out of me. A moment later he's running his fingers along my folds, murmuring something barely audible to my ears but sounds like *so fucking good* as he teases me by slipping a finger barely inside me, just enough to have me squirming, near begging for relief. My orgasm hovers like a helicopter above a landing pad.

"Whose pussy is this?" he asks, continuing to dip in and out of me. I whimper and thrust forward, chasing his fingers. Heats unfurls in my stomach when he crooks his finger inside me, hitting that spot that sends electricity zapping all over my skin. "Dandi."

I nearly wail when he removes his finger.

"Whose pussy is this?" he demands, landing another swat on my core.

"Objection," I pant, worried the sheets are now drenched in my arousal. "Leading the witness."

His snort of a laugh is lost when he enters me with two fingers, stretching me as he uses his tongue as a weapon of mass destruction. Fire licks down my spine as he finger fucks me into oblivion. My orgasm barrels towards me, liquid heat pouring into my veins and setting off explosion after explosion.

"Holy shit." I'm out of breath, lungs contracting as Win continues to move inside me, my inner walls still pulsing around his fingers. He draws another orgasm out of me as he puts more pressure on my g-spot, adding the suction of his mouth.

"Mmm." He groans. "Better than I remember."

I whimper when he pulls his fingers out of me. A slurping sound draws my attention to Win licking his fingers clean in the most erotic way. He climbs up my body and pins my arms above me, kissing me fiercely like if this is his only night with me, he's going to make it count. The taste of me on his tongue sends a shiver down my spine and detonates my nerve endings.

His teeth graze the skin of my neck, and he sucks hard enough I wouldn't be surprised if he left a mark. I'm throbbing all over, ready to climb him as he nips at the shell of my ear. Our gazes lock, and his morphs into a mysterious, alluring storm.

Chapter Ten
Win

One night. No strings.

She's beneath me, but my mind is a million miles in the future trying to figure out how to keep her. I can't let her go after one night. I've dreamt of this moment for longer than I care to admit, and as her taste lingers on my tongue and her warm body presses up against mine, I'll do anything to make sure she doesn't slip from my grasp.

We might've fallen into this situation because I needed a pretend girlfriend but make no mistake, I don't need to pretend to my Nana that Andi means more to me than my career. Andi is—and has always been—the person I care about most in this world.

Andi's tongue slides across my nipple, and her teeth clamp down, playfully tugging the piercing. My cock jerks at the sensation, and any apprehension I had about sleeping with my best friend's little sister—again—flies out the window when her firm grasp wraps around me.

"Andi," I groan, struggling not to thrust into her grip.

She pumps me twice with her lithe fingers before I pull away. After waiting years to touch her again, I refuse to be a two-pump-chump. Everything about this experience is different than when we were teens groping around in the dark and didn't realize pleasure wasn't from the release but from the build-up. I want to take my time with her, discover the meaning of every little sound she makes, and repeat it over and over again until she begs me to stop.

"Win." Her breath is wispy and light as she wiggles beneath me, brushing her fingers down my sides. My muscles flex from the soft tickle. "Do you have a condom?"

Of all the things I imagined I'd be doing tonight, searching my childhood nightstand for a condom that has probably been there since I graduated from high school would be last on the list. My fingers sweep along my old iPod, a tube of Carmex, and tangled up earbuds in search of the foil packet. Sweaty palms and a pounding heart make for frantic fumbling as I finally latch onto the condom.

Fuck, it's expired.

"Gimme a sec." I scurry out of the bed in search of my pants.

"Amateur," she quips with a smirk.

The cool air hits my ass, sending goosebumps along my skin as I snag the condom from my wallet. Back at the bedside, a glance at Andi shows me she's started the show without me. Her breasts are heavy in her hands, dusky nipples peaked and begging to be lavished. I swat her center as I roll the condom on with my other hand.

"Didn't I tell you to stop touching yourself?"

She moans and squirms beneath me, rubbing her thighs together. "I plead the fifth."

"I—" I smother the words that bubble up in laughter—ones I've longed to say for years that aren't a laughing matter. Only Andi can make lawyer jokes during sex and somehow, I find it more erotic than if she was screaming my name. I shove the emotions back to where they've sat dormant the past ten years and flip her over.

"Win!" she squeaks.

"Time to teach you a lesson." I lean over her back, and my cock settles between her juicy ass. I nip at the shell of her ear, tweaking her nipple as I say, "Head down, ass up."

"Excuse me?" Her voice is stunned, but she can't disguise the desire that flashes across her features.

Tingles spread out over my palm as I swat her right ass cheek, and her mewl sends a thrill straight to my cock.

"That's one for not listening the first time." I caress her soft skin, soothing the sting.

"I object." She thrusts her bottom back and I catch her hips.

"On what grounds?" I grit out, memorizing her curves with roving fingertips.

"Badgering the witness." She keens as my thumb coasts over the puckered rose of her behind.

"I'm going to make this ass sing twice more." I glide my fingertips along her smooth stomach and find her clit, drawing circles around the slick bud. "And then I'm going to fuck you like I should've done all those years ago."

She groans. "Stop talking and do—"

I deliver two quick spanks before she's finished her smart remark, this time soothing the pink skin with my mouth as my middle finger and thumb roll her clit. She shatters beneath me, goosebumps covering her skin when she cries out.

"You were saying?" I slide my finger through her release, dipping in and out of her entrance, teasing her as she rides out her orgasm.

She answers by pushing her ass toward me. My dick throbs as it slides between her legs, gathering her slickness. She gasps when I spread her, taking a handful of her ample ass.

"Whose ass is this?" I ask, thrusting along her sensitive folds.

"Yours," she says breathily, having learned her lesson.

"You're damn right." I notch my tip at her entrance. Precum beads the slit, balls drawing up in anticipation. The magnitude of the moment pulls my ribs tight, sending a flush of heat to my face as insecurities flood in.

"You sure about this?" I loathe the way I sound like a little boy, constantly needing affirmation that someone wants me, a reminder that I'm not in this alone. I once thought we were in this together, both on the same page about what was happening between us. I don't want to make the same mistake twice.

Andi stills beneath me, and I don't miss the way her body goes rigid a moment before she relaxes and looks over her shoulder at me with a smirk. "Scared you're gonna fall in love?"

As if I'm not already?

My stomach pitches at her deflection. I fight an inner battle on whether to respond playfully or truthfully. I wrap her hair around my fist and lean forward to nip at her ear. "Dandi, I fell in love ten years ago."

She rolls her eyes as if she doesn't believe me then opens her mouth, no doubt ready to spear me with her usual sarcasm. I don't give her time to respond. I thrust, sinking half inside her warmth. We both groan, and I draw in a shaky breath as heat unfurls at the base of my spine.

"Fuck," Andi sighs, wiggling to accommodate me. "You feel so good."

"That's only half, sweetheart." I chuckle, fighting the urge to thrust. My fingers ache as I dig into her hips, holding her still. A zing of pleasurable pain zips up my cock as she reaches between her legs and tugs on my balls. I slam home, seated fully inside her.

Breath whooshes out of me, and my knees nearly buckle. If I thought sex with Andi would be passionate and slow, I'd be wrong on many accounts. Our sweat slicked bodies turn animalistic, each fighting for dominance in this uncharted territory. She matches my drive, swiveling so her ass meets my groin.

My grunts and her moans mix to make the most erotic soundtrack, yet I struggle to hear anything except for the thundering pulse in my ears. I slow our pace and lift Andi, so she's pressed to my torso, giving me ample space to palm her breasts.

They're the perfect size, a fact I relay to the shell of her ear as I pinch her nipple. She wraps her arm around my neck, pulling me forward into a kiss. Each thrust is a wish I send to the universe, begging for more time with her. Her breath quickens as I find her clit, but I want to see her beautiful face when she comes apart.

She whines when I pull out and flip her onto her back, but I cover her mouth with mine, sensually tangling our tongues. With one pitch of my hips, I'm back inside her. Toned, brown legs wrap around my waist, ankles locked as she digs her heels into my butt, urging me forward. Long black eyelashes fan out over her shining toffee eyes, and she closes them as if I can't tell she's hiding her emotions.

"Look at me," I urge, not moving an inch. Her forehead crinkles and she squeezes them tighter. I grasp her chin and nibble on her plump pout. "Andi," I growl. "Open your eyes."

Ever the frustrating woman she is, she refuses. My mouth ticks up with a smile, secretly loving her feistiness. I lean back, her legs still wrapped around me and her core front and center. Almost unconscious of herself, she opens for me as if she anticipates what's coming. I trail my fingers across the smooth expanse of her soft stomach. "Last chance," I say.

"Please," she whispers.

Arousal courses through my veins, and I draw in a shaky breath as I land a swat to her slick core, relishing in the moan that escapes. Her eyes pop open, brown irises blown in pleasure. I slide inside her with no resistance, hitting a spot that makes her bite down on my shoulder.

Like music to my ears, the only sound in the room is our bodies moving together and her soft whimpers as she nears euphoria.

"Just like that." Her words are soft, delivered as if her throat is too tight to allow her vocal cords room to expand.

I stay where I'm at and pump twice more, taking note of the way Andi's mouth parts when I hit a certain spot. She grasps the disheveled sheets and digs her heels into my rear, inner walls clamping around me.

"Fuck," I drag out, unprepared for the tight hug of her pussy as it flutters around me. Sparks shoot off at the base of my dick, and my balls draw up, releasing every particle of my being into this moment.

I collapse onto the bed beside her, struggling to catch my breath. I don't speak for fear of allowing every emotion I'm keeping behind closed doors from flowing out in a pathetic post sex conversation. Letting Andi know that one night is not enough is a conversation best left for the morning when I can ply her with food and coffee.

"You know," she starts, pointing to the wall beside my door. "It should be illegal to fuck in a room where there are posters of N'SYNC and Stone-Cold Steve Austin still hanging on the wall."

I fight the urge to correct her. What we did wasn't just sex to me. It was me showing her that there's still something between us, something distance or time didn't affect. The love we shared all those years ago is still aflame inside us, and if she'd let it, I know it could become a roaring fire again.

I turn and stare down at her, swiping a lock of her curly hair out of her face. "I'm sorry the ambiance was lacking."

"Amongst other things," she sighs. I glare at her, and she cracks a wide grin before adding, "I'm just kidding, Win."

I grasp her face and pour every last feeling I have into our kiss. When we part, we're both breathless and my cock is already hard again. I curse high school me for not giving into the peer pressure to buy an entire box of Magnum's and silently promise my cock to never make that mistake again.

***

Pots clank loudly in the kitchen, and the sweet, smoky scent of bacon rouses me. I crack open an eye and immediately regret it. Bright light spills in from the curtains, reflecting off a heap of snow and searing my corneas. I should've closed them before I fell asleep with Andi in my arms but the thought of her nestled into my side, resting on my chest and leg thrown over my waist, brings a smile.

I slide my foot over, searching out her warmth beneath the covers. Cool air caresses my leg, and I try to turn over but find I'm stuck. Awareness settles over me, the tingling in my fingertips drawing my attention to the tinsel wrapped around my wrists, securing my arms to the bed.

"What the fuck," I whisper, tugging at the tinsel. It doesn't budge. What is she, the Chuck Norris of tying knots? Red and green flashes in my lower peripherals, and a glance at my pecs reveals two glittery Christmas bulbs attached to my nipple piercings.

"Andi," I growl and clench my jaw against the laugh trying to escape. Only she would find tying me to the bed and dressing me up like a Christmas tree funny.

I pour every ounce of strength I have into pulling the tinsel, praying my bicep workouts won't fail me. With a loud rip, one hand is free. I flex my numb fingers and shake the fuzziness away before releasing the other. For posterity's sake, I check my groin to make sure she hasn't managed to wrap a popcorn garland around my cock. Though the image of her eating the salty snack as she gobbles my dick isn't a bad one, it's not popcorn that I find.

I touch Andi's cool pillow. Is she still here? How long has she been gone?

Uncertainty wobbles insides me, a spinning top dancing through the memories. She said one night, but I'm having trouble believing she'd walk away after the way she kissed me and how our bodies fit together perfectly.

Sex doesn't erase the hurt you caused her, my mind helpfully supplies.

Though my brain knows it's right, my heart withers at the thought of losing Andi again. Nana's request that I value something other than material things before she retires rings loudly in my ears. I was an asshole teenager who didn't take care of things and people he loved. What if the one thing I don't have—the person I want the most—I still don't deserve?

My dad warped my mind so much I believed I wasn't worthy of anything good, that I'd eventually ruin things anyway. I've tried for years to become the type of man who earns what I have—the successful career, a house in a nice part of town, an expensive car.

Nausea roils my stomach as I trudge to the shower. Hot water beats the tension from my neck, sluicing down my body and highlighting the red marks across my abs. The memory of Andi's nails digging into my skin awakens my cock, saluting the tiles like a soldier ready for duty. Ever the masochist, I refuse to relieve the urge until I know whether she's left or not.

I towel dry, throw on a long sleeve Henley, and grab the sweats I wore last night before I think better of it. Sweatpants do not make for boner appropriate clothing. Instead, I snatch a pair of jeans from the closet, shoving my aching cock behind the denim.

Nana's husky laugh and the scent of cinnamon in the air beckons me down the hall. My mouth waters at the thought of soft, flaky pastry and sweet icing. I halt in the doorway of the kitchen, my breath catching at the sight of my three favorite women around the island.

She's still here.

None of them notice me, so I have ample time to watch. Beside Nana, Andi's hair is fastened back with a few wavy pieces scattered about her face, and the shirt I let her borrow is tied in a knot, baring the tiniest sliver of brown skin. She lifts her icing-covered fingers to her mouth and licks them, rousing the beast I tamed behind a zipper. Arousal floods my system, tingling all over my body.

Bright brown eyes land on me, and longing crowds my chest as she laughs at something my mom says. My movements are languid, unhurried as I approach and wrap my arms around her waist, pulling her into me. She melts in my embrace, and I swear Nana and Mom swoon behind us.

Andi looks over her shoulder. "Good morning."

Testing my luck, I tilt her chin and kiss her short and sweet since we're not alone. "Good morning, Munchkin." I lean closer to whisper. "Nice decorations this morning. I especially loved the candy cane hung on my dick." I nip at her ear. "I'll be returning the favor soon."

She blows air out of her nose like a cute bull, ready to charge. An elbow to the gut has me backing away with a smirk on my face. I greet my mom and Nana and slide onto a stool at the island.

"Cinnamon rolls?" I ask, pulling the sheet pan toward me to help Andi roll the pastries.

"Nothin' better on a chilly winter morning," Nana replies. "Had to teach your lady here how to make Nana's famous cinnamon rolls."

I watch for Andi's reaction to Nana calling her my lady, expecting her to flinch or frown at the phrase, but she doesn't. She smiles up at Nana and bumps her shoulder like they're old friends.

"Nana told me all about the time you tried to make your own cinnamon rolls but forgot the sugar." Her mouth quirks up and she covers her face to stifle a laugh.

With sticky fingers, I ball up a tiny piece of dough and fling it her way. It lands in her shirt, and her fists bunch like she's repressing the urge to punch me. Her glare makes me laugh.

"Winchester," Mom chastises and slides me a stack of plates and cutlery. "Go set the table."

Unwilling to let her out of my sight, I ensure Andi is seated next to me. We haven't talked about her leaving yet, so if this breakfast is the last little bit of time I have with her, I want her close enough to touch.

"What are you kids up to today?" Nana asks, sipping a steamy cup of coffee.

Hopefully the same stuff we were up to last night. I lock away the words I want to say as Andi's foot nudges mine beneath the table. She slides her leg against mine, and I grip her thigh, squeezing lightly.

"I have some work I need to finish before the holidays, so as long as the roads are passable, I'll probably leave after breakfast," Andi replies.

My lungs squeeze with a repressed sigh, and I fight a grimace. I'm not ready for this to be over—not ready to have her walk out of my life again.

The workshop in the unfinished basement pops into my mind. I'm sure my mom forgot about it since she keeps everything she needs on the shelving inside the garage, but it's the perfect excuse to keep Andi here longer.

"Would it be alright if she uses the tools in the basement?" I ask, hoping my mom can hear the pleading tone of my voice.

"Of course," she replies with a shrug. "Use whatever you need, Andi."

Andi's mouth curves up. "That's so sweet, Ms. Robinson. Thank you."

Mom swats the air. "Cut that Ms. Robinson stuff out. Call me Holly."

After a hearty breakfast of eggs, bacon, and gooey cinnamon rolls, Andi and I wash the dirty dishes, barely managing not to flick water at each other like children. Being around her again feels completely natural—like the last ten years never happened.

"Wanna check out the basement?" I ask, drying the last plate.

Andi's eyes sparkle at the mention of the workshop, and my heart squeezes knowing I can make her happy and support her in a way her family never has. It's an honor I'm not sure I deserve, but one I'll happily don.

Chapter Eleven

Andi

I cross and uncross my arms, nervously fidgeting as we near the steps to the basement. Last night was...amazing. More than I ever expected, considering the last time we were intimate was when we barely knew our own bodies. Somehow, the experience was new, yet familiar. We moved in tandem as we catalogued each other's curves, challenged for dominance over one another, and fell into sated bliss. My mound and butt still ache from the way he spanked me—something I never thought I'd enjoy—and my inner walls flutter thinking about him doing it again.

"Here we are," he stops in front of a door.

My gaze flits to the entrance with a mixture of excitement and apprehension. A workshop is exactly what I need—the entire reason I came back to work at my grandparent's bakery—but it also reminds me that this thing between us is just a...deal.

Last night when he asked me what we were doing, my mind froze. How was I supposed to tell him that I wanted more than one night with him when the only reason we were even in this situation was because he *needed* me to pretend to be his? On the phone, while we were putting up the decorations, I overheard my brother ask him about finding a date for Nana's arrival. It wasn't like I didn't know about it, but my heart still twisted like he wrapped barbed wire around it.

I've kept my heart encased in a glass of ice, only having surface-level relationships because the last person I let in was him. The walls I built were to keep people out, but after last night, I realize all I did was lock him up tight inside, hoping that one day things could be different. But I was kidding myself to think that last night was real, that I was something more than just a warm body for the night and an actor there to convince his grandmother he cared about more than his career.

"It needs to be cleaned some," Win says. "But I think it'll work for what you need."

I look up, immediately aware how close we are. Memories of his body hovering over me, thrusting at just the right angle to make my toes curl, flash through my mind. His decadent mouth showering me with praise and dirty words in equal measure, drawing out every bit of pleasure. How I ever thought one night would be enough is beyond me.

I manage to squeak out, "Thank you for this."

His nose grazes the shell of my ear and my pulse skyrockets and then dives like a bird catching a fish. "You can thank me for it later."

Dazed, I miss him opening the door. A cool breeze chills my bare ankles, and I snap out of the cloud of arousal and follow him down the stairs. Light flickers somewhere in the dark room, illuminating the boxes stacked on either side like a maze. I follow the yellow orb, skirting past opened boxes filled with old China and weathered pictures, making it into the hidden corner where a large wooden table sits.

"Would this work for you?" Win asks, dusting off the top. "There's a ton of wood over in that barrel."

The earthy scent of pine floats into my nose, and I inhale a deep breath, comforted by the familiar smell. Pegboards filled with all types of screwdrivers, hammers, wrenches, and other various tools hang on the wall in pristine condition. The gleaming tools are a stark difference to my decade-old whittling set. My dad's voice rings in my ears, telling me my business is just a hobby and that I shouldn't needlessly spend money.

Dad didn't think women should be toiling all day, covered in dust, and Mom scoffed at the idea of spending money on something that wasn't dresses, ballet classes, or Botox. Appearances are everything to them.

My dreams weren't important—I wasn't important.

"Dandi?" A chill skitters up my arm as Win's cool fingertips graze the exposed skin.

I blink away the memory. Hoping he doesn't notice my wet lashes, I paste on a smile and turn toward the pile of wood. "This is perfect."

He grips my waist and spins me around, nudging my chin to look up at him, but I can't.

"What's wrong?" he asks, voice gentle and comforting.

My tongue is gummy in my mouth as I struggle to form words that won't make me look so...pathetic. Win knows what my parents are like, knows that Solo is the favored child who never had to ask for anything. I understand it's not my brother's fault he was born with a penis and therefore the keys to our parents' heart, but it doesn't help that he never once stood up for me when they were being unfair.

"I appreciate you letting me use the tools," I supply with a hoarse tone. My fingers twitch with the desire to get working on my orders. "They're in much better condition than my set."

"Then get to work, Dandi." A firm swat on my ass makes my skin flush with heat. His smile is sly and mischievous as he backs up the stairs. The door closes with a thwack, and my shoulders relax as I learn the setup. There's enough wood for me to cut down small enough to whittle my gnomes.

Pulling up my Etsy dashboard, I scroll through the orders and look at the details before I get to work. Each gnome can be personalized, or the customer can order the one I've deemed as the "Head Over Heels" garden gnome—my favorite order to complete. A twelve-inch high, upside-down gnome with a cone-shaped hat with a curl on top, a long flowy beard, shirt and shoes, and a sunflower in its hand. It represents the moment I tripped over that garden gnome and realized I was head over heels—literally—for Win.

I scroll through my queue, landing on a personalized order with multiple gnome hats stacked on sunflowers. I sigh with relief. Whittling the hats is the easiest part. The swooping curves of gnome bodies and hands are difficult to whittle, requiring a variation of push and pull strokes and stop cuts, and looking at the setup, there's no oblique knife I could use to carve those intricacies.

Hours pass in a blur of sawdust and basswood shavings. There's a slight cramp in my right hand, but my entire being vibrates with elation. I didn't realize how tense I was until I was able to get lost in the one thing that brought me peace. The contented feeling spreads over my body as my creative well refills.

Something shifts behind me, and I slowly turn to find Win in one of those uncomfortable fold-out chairs, relaxed in an unnatural angle sure to bring a crick to his neck. He must've snuck back inside when I was in the zone and fallen asleep. I take a moment to study him—a day ago, he was a boy, my villain, and today he's my savior. If someone had told me I'd be purposefully spending time with Winchester Robinson—and longing to spend a lot more with him—I would've laughed in their face. But last night showed me that as much as I'd like to deny it, my heart has only ever wanted him.

His thick, jean-clad legs are spread wide, long arms crossed in front of his body. Toned biceps straining beneath a cream-colored Henley. A smile skirting his face, even in sleep. I'm curious what he's thinking about, if he's reminiscing on last night and wondering if he—if we—made a mistake.

I hope not, because I've yet to build the courage to broach the conversation of what happens next. Because there's got to be more, right? The connection is still there. I can't be the only one who feels it like a fiery lasso wrapped around my core.

"Stop staring at my cock," he grumbles, sitting up and stretching out his neck.

"Keep dreaming." My entire face flames, but I stand firm and cross my arms, finding the playful nature between us easiest to fall back on. The storm might've been the reason we ended up in this situation, but surely once the roads are clear and I go back to Grams, he'll forget about our passion-filled night. "I'd need a magnifying glass to do that."

He scoffs and unfolds himself from the chair. My pulse thumps loudly in my ears when he prowls toward me, drinking in every feature on my face. His tongue darts out to moisten his lips, and my core clenches with the memory of his face between my legs, his beard scratchy along my thighs.

He slides his thumb along the border of my mouth. "Sounds like you need to get reacquainted then."

My thoughts scatter, rendering me speechless. I struggle to focus as need floods my system, but my hands take on a mind of their own. Firm, long, and trapped behind denim, I find his erection and squeeze. His groan rumbles against me, hitchhiking down to my core.

I draw from the confidence I managed to store while back in my creative zone, and say, "If I remember correctly, you said something about missing my smart mouth?"

A breath whooshes out of him, lifting the hairs that escaped my messy bun. He snatches the tie from my hair, sliding strong fingers through my tresses. He pulls me to him, our lips meeting in an explosive kiss. Teeth clinking, tongue sucking, lip biting. I grasp at his shirt, but the damn thing is too tight for his firm pecs, so I settle for digging my fingers into his chest.

Win steps back and flicks open the button on his jeans. The loss of his overwhelming presence is like a rug being pulled out from under me.

"On your knees, Dandi."

My nipples swell at the commanding tone in his voice. On any other occasion, being bossed around would irritate me, but the way my pussy just clenched at his order shows me this is not one of those times.

Win catches my arm when I begin to lower, halting me. I stare at him confused as he grabs a pillow from one of the boxes and places it on the ground for my knees. Win worrying about the state of my knees while he fucks my mouth shouldn't make hearts appear in my eyes, but it does.

I'm a goner.

"What if someone walks in?" I glance over his shoulder as if someone can see us in the corner behind all these boxes.

"Then I'd charge them five dollars for the show." He grins and swipes the pad of his thumb along my lips. "Open."

I suck on his thumb as he drops his pants, his erection bouncing against my stomach. With a pop, I release his finger and sink to my knees. I'm on fire as I stare down the thick, veiny titan. My insides flutter with the memory of him hitting the exact spot I needed him to over and over again, but there's a tiny voice in the back of my mind telling me there's no way I can fit even half of that in my mouth.

"Hold on." He reaches into his pocket, crinkling some kind of paper. I back up, momentarily confused until he hangs a peppermint candy cane on his erection. "Don't stop sucking until the red is gone."

Challenged accepted.

Excitement pings around my stomach, and I inhale a large breath and set my shoulders. I give his balls a light squeeze, relishing in the noise that slips from his mouth. Precum beads the head, and I flick my tongue over his slit and the candy cane, gathering the sweet and salty fluid. I wrap my hand around his girth and lick the pulsing line along his shaft.

"Fuck," he groans, jerking as if I've hit a ticklish spot. Can dicks be ticklish?

Sensitive.

I chuckle at my idiocy, and Win—probably thinking I'm making a joke about his dick—pitches his hips forward, touching the back of my throat. I gag on his length and the candy cane, but I'm spurred on to make him weak in the knees. I hollow out my cheeks and suck him hard. The corners of my mouth are sticky and need throbs between my legs at his feral moan. I squeeze my thighs together to stem the ache of wanting him. Gentleman that he is, he thrusts shallowly in my mouth so I can breathe.

I draw him back inside, stroking the base of his cock and smiling at his sharp intake of breath when I pull back and a string of pink saliva connects my lips to his girth.

"Your mouth was made to take my cock," he husks out, tipping my chin up so my teeth graze his sensitive skin. I'm soaked, not only from his words but from the high of hearing him panting like he can't draw a full breath.

He shivers, and a devious grin works its way onto my face when I find the candy cane nearly stripped white. I inch my finger backward and glide it along the taut skin behind his heavy sack. He grips my scalp and tugs me up, bathing me in wet kisses as the candy falls and shatters on the ground.

"Tell me you want this." He lavishes my neck, sucking on the skin on my collarbone with such force I know he's left a mark. "One night isn't enough. You fucking know it isn't."

Hearing him parrot my thoughts back to me flips the latch on the dam holding the feelings I've kept closed up tight. Something blooms in the pit of my stomach at his words, his insinuation that there's more here.

"It'll never be enough," I whimper as we meet in a combustible kiss.

He works the button on my jeans, and within seconds they're on the floor and pushed to the side.

"No panties," he chuckles darkly, knowing he ripped them last night. He hoists me up against the unpainted drywall and opens his mouth to ask for permission, but I beat him to it by saying, "I'm on the pi—"

He's inside me before I finish, stealing my breath with a thrust that has him seated and me biting my lip so hard I taste blood. He curses into my neck, panting and grunting like a caveman as he unspools me.

We both look down at where we're connected, drunk on the heady mixture of torment and ecstasy. He pulls out and teases the soaked juncture between my thighs before squeezing the globes of my ass as an anchor. The erotic slap of our flesh fills the room, and fire tears through me as his hips switch between piston-like strokes and circles to hit my G-spot.

"Win...Win," I whimper as the orgasm builds. "I need more."

"Anything for you," he replies, our sweat-slicked bodies moving like a symphony. "Wrap your arms around my neck and don't let go." He nudges my nose, pulling my gaze toward him. "That's an order."

I bask in his dominance and the reverent way he touches me. He knows what my body needs and isn't afraid to give it to me, and for once, I'm not afraid to give him the reins.

"Ok, Judge," I reply, securing my hands around his neck. His traps are firm, the perfect armrests.

Win wraps an arm around my waist and pins me flush against the drywall, his cock buried deep inside me. Fingertips glide up my leg, squeezing ever so lightly as he hitches my knee around his waist. His hand is back on my ass within seconds, but it doesn't stop there.

Lava pours into my veins when he spreads me and the pad of his finger swipes across the puckered entrance between my cheeks.

"Win." My voice is thin and reedy, and my heart pounds furiously all over my body. It's not until I earn a slap to the ass that I realize I've unwound my hands from his neck.

"Be a good girl," he says, pulling far enough out of me that his tip meets my clit. "Keep those arms around my neck."

The way my pussy flutters when he swats my ass compels me to be disobedient, but I crave my orgasm more than my next breath. I nod, tilting my hips and taking his cock deeper. He groans against my neck and tweaks my nipple over my bra cup. My inner walls squeeze him, and it unlocks the beast.

"Perfect...mine...heaven," he murmurs as his finger inches back between my legs. He gathers my arousal, and with tender care he broaches the tight ring of muscle. I suck in a sharp breath, squirming as I get used to the full feeling. "You okay?"

Words evade me, replaced by a feeling of euphoria. I'm lost to the endorphins rushing through my body and the thud of my heart in my ears. There's nothing but this moment, this man, this...all-encompassing contentedness swirling in the air.

"So...so good," I reply.

With a playful smirk, he gets back to business, pumping in both places like a seesaw. His cock. His finger. His tongue in my mouth. Every sense I have overtaken by him. My orgasm builds, ebbing and flowing, before sending a tidal wave of euphoria through me. Win follows me over the hill, thrusting three more times before he releases hot jets of cum inside me.

I'm a boneless heap, barely able to stand as he sets my legs on the ground. Win gathers the warm liquid slipping down my thigh with his other hand and pushes his fingers back inside me. "Let's put that back where it belongs."

"Who the hell are you?" I laugh, fighting for air like I'm suffocating. Since the moment he stepped into Grams's bakery, every encounter between us feels like it's been ripped from one of those romance books my mom thinks she has hidden in her office.

On bended knee, Win taps my calf, helping me into my discarded skinny jeans. I'm sticky and in need of a shower, but I also never want to wash his touch from my body.

"Thank you," I breathe out as he secures his still semi-hard dick behind his zipper. Unease about where we go from here ferments in my gut, and I blurt out, "For letting me use the tools." Internally, I facepalm, but outwardly, I make it even more awkward by adding, "And the orgasms."

His brows bunch and his shoulders shake with a laugh. "Your pleasure's all mine, Andi."

I don't miss the way he personalizes the statement. Turning from him, I clean up the work desk so he can't see all the questions battering my mind. I've always been independent, but most would call me emotionally distant. It's not on purpose, it's a knee-jerk reaction to protect myself from hurt I know is coming. I could ask him if he wants to see where this could go, but he's made it pretty clear he's only looking for sex. His focus is on his career, and this thing between us is what he needs to move forward in that. Once I leave this house—this bubble of lust we've created—I'll go back to working in the bakery, saving up to rent a new workshop after Win helps me sue my landlord. And Win will get the promotion he deserves.

Exactly the deal we decided on.

Chapter Twelve
Win

My mind is a ball of yarn being batted around by an imaginary cat. Watching Andi in her zone, whittling away at her gnomes, fills me with so much love. I could sit and watch her work for hours. The way her forearms flex as she carves the wood into submission, the lithe movement of her hips as she dances to songs only she can hear, and the sheer happiness on her face when she holds her work up to the light and nods as if she's telling herself 'good job'.

I love her.

Still.

I pray silently, thanking God for my meddling Nana—and the snowstorm. Too many things needed to align for Andi to find her way back to me. Nana's declaration that I needed to find value in my life, my mom ordering a cake from Grams's bakery, Andi's car trouble, and my Nana's early arrival all fell into place in a way that seems like something bigger than me is pulling the strings, begging us to find our way back to each other.

Permanently.

"Were you able to finish all your orders?" I ask, peeking over Andi's shoulder as she finishes cleaning the desk.

She shrugs. "No, but I got enough done to feel like I'm on track. I'll figure out a way to finish the rest once I go back home."

I frown, not wanting to think about her leaving after all that's happened between us. Did I not show her how good we could be together? Have I not done enough good to truly deserve her? Or is the past too big a chasm for her to leap?

Now that Nana is here and we've chatted some about her retirement, I don't feel the need to stay and convince her anymore. Andi could simply come back to my house, and we could continue working out whatever this is between us.

I just have to build the courage to ask.

"I...I should get going," she says, staring at the ground.

My shoulders fall, and my heart plummets.

I guess that answers my unasked question.

I spin on my heels and walk back through the maze of boxes, keeping my back to her so she can't see my crestfallen expression. The backs of my eyes prickle, but I ignore the sensation. I should be thankful that I got more than just one night to hold her, to pretend that she was truly mine.

"Did the setup work out for you, Andi?" My mom asks as we enter the kitchen. Snow falls in thick flakes outside the window behind Nana where the bright light has now faded to an array of gray and purple hues.

"It was exactly what I needed. Thank you so much," Andi says.

"Coffee?" Nana raises an empty cup.

"Andi likes tea," I chime in just as Andi says, "I should probably get going before the storm worsens."

An awkward tension hangs in the air at our miscommunication, and it's Nana who breaks the silence.

"Pish posh." She waves off Andi's statement. "I'm making eggplant parmigiana. You've got to stay for dinner!"

There's no way she'll be able to stay for dinner and make it back to Grams's house before the roads are too slick to drive. Part of me wonders if Nana asked that question in hopes that it'll force Andi to stay another night, to give us one more chance to make things right. To actually talk with our mouths instead of our bodies. My brain is saying *please, please, please*, but outwardly, I hold my breath and raise my eyebrows at her in question.

"I'd love to," she replies.

Her smile as she looks at me jolts through my body, severing the string anchored to my heart. It floats around my chest, filling every nook and cranny with love for her. The longer she stays and keeps up this ruse, the harder it's going to be when she eventually leaves, but I can't help but be greedy with the time afforded to me.

Within these four walls, it's easy to believe I deserve her and that she could still love a man like me.

"Can you teach me how to make it?" Andi asks, sliding onto a stool.

Nana's face lights up. "Of course, Puddin'."

Appreciation anchors me to this moment, watching the woman I always dreamed I'd have a life with, being taught our family recipe by my grandmother. My pulse thumps all over my body as Andi eagerly leans across the table.

Nana launches into step-by-step instructions and, relieved Andi's staying, I take an hour to check on emails and return phone calls. While she slept, I reached out to some contacts from the Better Business Bureau to check on the man Andi was renting her space from. A brief look at the results shows me he has a poor track record, one that makes it easy to follow the trail of what's going on behind the scenes. Feeling confident I have everything to help her, I return to the kitchen where the aroma of fresh garlic and tomato sauce call to me.

Nana warms to Andi, taking her under her wing like the granddaughter she never had. Brown hair swept back into a low bun, a red apron secured tight around her ample curves, flour streaked across her cheek, Andi looks perfect. Her fitting in so well with my family only makes my heart squeeze painfully because I'll never be accepted into hers.

Hell, she's not even accepted into hers, my mind supplies. It's true, but I don't want to be the cause of further estrangement between her and her family.

They fall into an easy back-and-forth conversation, chatting about how Andi got started in carpentry. Nana, being the hardworking woman she is, grills Andi on her business plans. With each curveball, Andi knocks it out of the park.

"What was my grandson *really* like in high school?" Nana asks, placing a pot of water to boil on the stove.

I'm suddenly hyper-focused on the words about to leave Andi's mouth. My pulse throbs and the base of my neck tingles when her gaze lands on me perched up against the entrance.

"Everyone thought he was a bad boy," she says, using air quotes. "Every girl wanted to date him, and every boy wanted to be him."

Her words, meant to be a compliment about my prowess, strike a chord of regret. I never wanted to be the 'bad boy.' I was lost, angry, and felt like no one cared about me. Mom was always at work, Nana lived too far, and I had no guidance. Drugs, vandalism, graffiti, they were all an escape from feelings I couldn't handle. I did whatever I wanted and didn't care what anyone thought. Other's opinions about me could never be worse than what I felt about myself.

Nana frowns. Andi doesn't realize it, but she's not helping my case for promotion by reminding my grandmother of my poor decisions.

"But they didn't know him," Andi continues. "They saw tattoos and piercings and assumed things about him that weren't true."

My ears perk up, gaze drawn to the woman smiling back at me.

"They didn't know how smart or kind he was, how he helped me pass my social studies class when I couldn't remember anything about the justice system." She swipes a rogue piece of hair out of her face. "And how he makes the best cup of tea."

A smile returns to Nana's face, and I imagine if she had x-ray vision, all she'd see are tattered pieces floating in the air where my heart just exploded. Despite wondering if she's only saying those things because of our deal, I'm convinced it's because those moments still mean something to her. If I can show her that I'm still the same boy she fell for, then maybe we can move forward. I open my mouth to respond when the doorbell rings.

"I'll get it." I unfold from the doorway and steal one last look at Andi. She's smiling and happy, and I want nothing more than to keep her that way.

The fireplace crackles inside the living room, warming my bare feet as I pad to the front door. Wine glasses are still perched on the coffee table, and I'm hit with the memory of kissing Andi last night. A shift in the tectonic plates of our previously rocky relationship. My cock throbs knowing less than an hour ago we were connected, a gift I never expected. The ferocity of her kisses, the way she digs her fingers and toes into me when she's on the cusp of her release, and her little mewls are part of the movie reel I'll play in my mind when she eventually leaves.

The glass panes beside the wooden door are foggy and wet with condensation, blocking my view of the person at the door. They're dressed in a large, puffy red coat, shifting back and forth on their feet as they wait for me to answer. It's likely one of the neighborhood kids asking if we want them to shovel the snow from the driveway, no doubt trying to save up money for a new sled or snowmobile.

I exhale a frustrated breath and paste a welcoming smile onto my face. Snowflakes fall to the dark cherry floor as I open the door, and my mouth drops when I find the last person I want to see standing in front of me.

Chapter Thirteen
Andi

"He's changed so much since high school," I say, stirring the fresh pasta Nana showed me how to make. "Seeing his face all over billboards and bus benches was a surprise."

Win's mom snorts as she chops romaine for a Caesar salad. "He hates those billboards."

I smile at that. Win's definitely the type to hide any time a camera is around. Having his face plastered all over Massachusetts is equivalent to a root canal for him.

"He's the face of the company." Nana drains the pasta in a colander. "People need to see a face they can trust, one that pops into their head when they need a lawyer."

Even though I never would've reached out to him for advice had I not gotten stranded in the snowstorm, I understand the sentiment. The more people see you, the more they trust you.

A familiar voice in the distance makes my knees nearly buckle. "Oh, no," I whisper with a sour taste in my mouth. My heartbeat slugs as the dread settles in. Of all the people who could've come to the door, my brother is the last person I expected.

I drop the colander filled with pasta in the sink and inhale a deep breath. "I'll be right back." I leave the kitchen and inch toward the front door. Staying out of sight, I sneak into the hallway wall to listen.

"What are you doing here?" Win asks, his voice tight.

I hold my breath, listening for Solomon's answer. "You didn't show up last night, and when I called you sounded weird then hung up on me. Figured I'd check on you to make sure you were alright."

Win snorts out a laugh. "I guess I should be happy you didn't drive over last night to check on me."

"Nah, man. The snow was too bad, so I passed out on Mina's couch after the bar."

I struggle to hear Win's response, wondering if he's telling Solo we had a similar situation happen. Even though we're both consenting adults, Solo finding his sister and his best friend together—with our tumultuous past—is not going to bode well for me or Win. But I want—need—to know what this is between me and Win before everyone else moves in to tell us what it shouldn't be.

Not only that, but I have yet to tell my parents or brother what happened with my landlord, and they're already waiting for me to fail.

Please, get him to go home.

"Solomon Johnson," Win's mom exits the kitchen, figuratively blowing up any chance of my brother leaving without more prompting.

Win sucks in a sharp breath, and I can imagine the glare he's giving his mom right now. I should've left earlier when I said I was going to, shouldn't have tempted fate by stealing more time in this happy place where we could just be, outside of the expectations of others and the bad memories.

"Miss Holly," Solomon replies in a saccharine voice. "You look lovely as ever, not a day over forty."

"Hey man," Win starts. "Stop hitting on my mom."

Solomon laughs loudly, and I collapse against the wall as I stare at the clock that says it's nearly three o'clock. Christmas time is supposed to be filled with magic, but thus far all I've had is bad luck. I lost my workshop, my car broke down, and now the little bubble of peace and happiness I found in all of that is about to be popped. While it may be a Christmas miracle that Win and I found forgiveness—and something else I can't quite figure out—there's still the issue of convincing his Nana we're together.

We can't fool my brother. If Solomon sees I'm here and blows our cover, Win's chance at becoming a partner is at risk. I can't let that happen.

"It's been too long since I've seen you, boy." Nana's voice floats through the air, and I curse beneath my breath. "My eggplant parmigiana is almost finished. Stay for dinner."

No, no, no. The hair all over my body rises, the prickles itchy as my pulse skyrockets. I wish I could see Win's face right now. Their footsteps and voices crescendo the closer they get to me, and my gaze bounces to the opened bathroom door. Three steps and I could be safe inside the bathroom to meltdown.

"I'd love to," Solomon replies, detonating a bomb inside my chest.

Shadows pass through the light emanating from the kitchen, and I peek around the corner, catching Win's furrowed brows and slumped posture behind my brother. I discreetly wave to catch Win's attention, and the way his chin dips and his arms hang limply at his sides show me he's unsure what to do.

Nausea churns in my gut, and I stumble to the bathroom, splashing cool water against my face. I stare in the mirror, surprised to see something like happiness sparkling in my eyes. Growing up as a pastor's kid, with parents who feel women are best seen not heard, propped up in the kitchen while the men work, I never understood what true happiness was. Though my craft shop is successful enough that I can rent an apartment in a nice part of town, when I go home at the end of the night, there's still only one set of dishes that ever need washing.

I thought I was okay with that, with the fact that I don't have someone waiting at home for me and that my family doesn't come to visit. But after spending one night in the comfort of Win's arms, and the warmth and love of his family, I yearn for it.

I can't let Solomon ruin that.

Not knowing what's going on in Win's mind is enough to drive me crazy. I know we play around about Solomon chopping off his balls, but there's a serious chance this thing between us could blow up in both of our faces and he could lose the only friend he's had for years. I don't want to be the reason that happens, yet I can't help but want him to finally fight for us the way he didn't last time.

Inside the kitchen, Solomon chats with Win's mom about his cyber-security business. I force steel into my spine and draw my shoulders back, schooling my face into a picture of relaxation.

"Andi?" Solomon's voice rises in pitch. "What're you doing here?" Before I have a chance to tell him about helping at the bakery he asks, "Why didn't you tell me you were in town?"

All the courage I mustered up in the bathroom drains from my body. I look to Win, waiting for him to show me in some way what I'm supposed to say. Do I tell my brother the truth? Do I even know what that is at this point? Last night was one of the best nights of my life, an eye-opening experience that healed parts of me I didn't know were still raw. But they left me with more questions that I don't know how to answer.

"Her car broke down and she needed a ride home," he says, gaze drifting to the snow that has picked up outside the window.

A crease forms on Solomon's brow. "This doesn't look like home to me."

Everyone's stare settles on me, and my knee rapidly bounces beneath the table. Last night, we told his Nana and mom that we wanted to keep the relationship between us because we wanted to get to know each other again without everyone else's opinions weighing on us but standing in front of my brother, I can't formulate a response that doesn't sound like a lie.

"There was no way she was going to make it home once they closed the streets," Nana chimes in, a look crossing her face that I can't quite pin down.

"Yeah," Win adds. "We were halfway to your grandparent's house when the sheriff detoured us. We would've been stranded in the storm had we kept going."

Suspicion laces my brother's features as his eyes bounce between us. Thankfully, Win's mom asks my brother a question about his work that has him forgetting all about this weird exchange.

"Can you guys grab two stools from the garage?" she asks, giving us an out, a moment to reset on this story she knows we've concocted. I'm not sure if he told his mom the truth, but after that knowing look and how she glances off to the hallway in an order, I assume the jig is up.

Nana keeps my brother chatting, so he doesn't see us slip out into the hallway. Win follows me closely, and I nearly squeal when he squeezes my butt.

"Stop it," I chide, batting him away.

"He's not paying attention," Win says, playfully cupping my breast when he reaches for the garage doorknob. Brisk air floats along my ankles as we step inside the garage, and within seconds I'm pressed up against the wall with Win devouring my mouth. His tongue sweeps along my bottom lip, and he takes the split second when I moan to dip inside and taste the sound trapped in my throat.

"You're going—" I blurt out when he gives me a moment of reprieve. "—to get us—" Win nips at my lip, his grasp moving to squeeze my waist. "—in trouble."

"Mmm," he hums, planting a kiss at the corner of my mouth. "We won't get caught."

I push against his shoulders, seeking space. While Win might be sure we won't be exposed, I'm thinking ahead to what happens when we are. This thing between us is still new—fragile—and the last thing I want is for Solomon to butt in and ruin things before they have a chance to bloom.

"We've gotta get him outta here," I say. "Or he's going to ruin everything."

The space between us must give Win a moment of clarity because he nods in understanding and backs away. "I'll figure out how to get him outta here after dinner."

He grabs the chair and kisses me one more time before returning inside. I take a moment to check that my hair isn't messed up. When I'm sure nothing is amiss, I follow, listening to my brother's booming laughter. Solomon has always had that certain *je ne sais quoi* when it comes to people, the ability to gather everyone around him and entertain. Though I can tell by Win's tight shoulders and how he barely seems to be breathing that he's on edge. Nana is enraptured in a tale Solomon is weaving about some risqué photos that were found on a senator's hard drive, and my gaze keeps flicking between my brother and my...Win.

Can we make it through this dinner without Solomon or Nana catching onto us?

Chapter Fourteen
Win

Solo's laugh is the soundtrack throughout dinner as he charms my mom and Nana, and I sit beside him covered in sweat with my stomach clenching each time we veer close to a topic that could reveal our deceit. Andi's face is relaxed as she joins the conversation, sliding her foot against mine beneath the table, though her fingers are tight around her fork as she takes a bite of eggplant. I can't help the way my gaze is drawn to her mouth as it closes around the tines, the working of her jaw as she chews, and the slow roll of her neck as she swallows.

It's sensual in a way that has my lower half waking up at the most inappropriate time.

A light chuckle jerks my attention to where everyone is staring at me, some with wide pupils and others with bunched brows. I don't spend too much time examining their expressions for fear that it'll pique more interest in my reaction.

"I'm sorry. Repeat that," I say, hopeful someone asked me a question.

"Did everything work out with that wrongful death case?" Solo asks.

I nod, twirling my pasta around my fork. "Yeah, the client ended up with a nice settlement and forced the company to implement new rules to prevent someone else from losing a loved one."

Solo fist pumps in the air as I take a bite. "Hell yeah, man. Better watch out, Nana. Win is coming for your record."

I choke on the eggplant, coughing through my shock. As good as his intentions are with trying to hype me up to Nana, the last thing I want is to draw attention to the stipulation she set forth.

Nana's smoky laugh eases my nerves. "My grandson might win on a basketball court, but he couldn't touch me in a court of law."

Dinner passes with relaxing conversation, and it's not until all of our phones get an emergency alert that the sinking feeling returns to my stomach.

Andi swipes her screen. "Ten-car accident."

I immediately look out the window at the dark skies filled with fat, falling snowflakes. Time flew by as we ate and Nana told us about how she and my grandfather started the law firm, and I barely noticed it's nearly seven o'clock.

"Where?" Solo grabs his own phone.

Nana and Mom continue eating, unphased by the sudden tension in the room. Accidents are an everyday occurrence when there is snow on the ground, and while a ten-car accident isn't unheard of, it's usually a bunch of small fender benders that can be cleared easily with a few tow trucks. But the way Andi's worried gaze flicks up to me confirms our night is about to take a turn for the worse.

"Pileup involving a tanker," she says with a grimace. *Please don't be the freeway Solo needs.* "Right before the 2/95 interchange."

Damn it.

I close my eyes briefly, letting the curses fly internally for a moment before I open them and find Solo staring back at me with a wide smile.

"Sleepover," he says, lounging into his chair. "Just like old times."

"Just like old times," I repeat, somehow managing not to directly look at Andi when I excuse myself to refill my drink in the kitchen and gather my thoughts. This is not how I imagined the rest of my evening going. I wanted to convince Andi to stay one more night, but now we're in this weird position where we have to keep up appearances around Nana yet stay far enough away from each other so that Solomon doesn't catch on.

If it was up to me, I'd tell Solo about us, but I'm not sure Andi is ready to handle his reaction yet.

Inside the kitchen, I fill my water and lean against the counter. Andi's laughter can be heard from the other room as dishes clash together, and a moment later she enters through the swinging door with arms full of dirty plates. I grab the wobbly tower from her and place it into the sink.

"What are we gonna do?" she whispers.

"My bed isn't big enough for the three of us."

She playfully pinches my arm. "That's not funny."

"What? You don't think he'd like the N'SYNC and Stone Cold posters too?" I regret the comment almost immediately, suffering through a punch to the kidney. "Okay, okay Apollo Creed."

"Be serious, Win." She moves toward the pantry, then stops and glances at the doorway to make sure no one is coming. "Remember the last time Solo ran his mouth before thinking?"

"Fine." I relent, turning on the water and dousing the dishes in soap. She's right. Solo has a big ass mouth, and it usually tends to get Andi in trouble with her parents. If she isn't ready to go up against them yet, I'll oblige her request to keep this between us. "Me and Solo can sleep down here in the living room and you can take the bedroom."

She nods. "That might work. I'll say goodnight now and go to bed, and you ask Solo if he wants to grab a beer and watch TV or something."

She tries to pass me, but I steal a quick kiss before she returns to the dining room and tells everyone goodnight. Within a few moments a door closes in the hallway, allowing me to finally relax. I finish washing the dishes and tidy up some as Nana doles out pieces of the cake I picked up from Grams's bakery. I think about taking a piece to Andi, but decide against it. It'll look too suspicious to Solomon.

I wish I could feed her this cake and lick the icing off her lips.

The orange-anise cake is the perfect finish to our dinner. Nana tells Solo goodnight as mom and I grab extra pillows and blankets from the linen closet. Mom's gaze heats the side of my face, willing me to confess to Nana and my best friend, but like the idiot I am, I ignore it. I'm not ready for our bubble to be popped yet.

Solo stretches out on the sofa while I find a less-than-comfy place on the rug in front of the fireplace. We watch TV in comfortable silence, only stopping to rib each other about who was better at a certain sport as a kid and who would win in the competition now that we're older. If it wasn't for Andi being all alone in my bed—something I keep telling myself to stop thinking about or I'm going to cave and spill the beans—I'd be enjoying this time with my best friend.

After drinking three beers and watching *Friday*, Solo's snores are the only thing I can hear over the crackling fireplace. I try to sleep, tossing and turning in the glow of the fire, but each time I'm almost there a certain brown-haired beauty pops into my mind. Is she asleep already? Is she wearing my clothes to bed again? Is she writhing behind her fingers as she imagines it's me?

I quietly groan, angry at my brain for conjuring the image.

My ears perk up at the soft click of a door handle and footsteps padding down the hallway. I glance over at Solo and find him damn near drooling. A moment passes before I hear a fork clink against something and Andi's soft curse.

My girl.

I nearly throw the cover into the fireplace getting off the floor. I kick it back toward my pillow and sneak into the kitchen. Andi's hair is loose down her back, and she's in my oversized white tee and a pair of gray sweatpants that hug her in just the right places. I inch closer, already smelling the fresh citrus scent I've come to associate with her. Her hips sway as she puts another bite into her mouth, and I slide up behind her and cover her mouth so she doesn't squeal. She forces her butt back, brushing against the erection I've been fighting to tame all evening.

"I would've brought you a piece." I brush her hair over her shoulder, placing a kiss at the junction of her neck and collarbone. She shivers and spins in my arms, standing on tiptoes to look over my shoulder before she kisses me back. Within seconds she deepens the kiss, and I groan at the flavors she's transferring from her tongue to mine.

"I want you," she moans into my mouth.

I pull her against me, so she can feel how much I agree with that statement. I think about taking her back to bed, giving her body the attention it deserves, spending the time we have left between her legs drawing out every moment of her pleasure until she's a pile of goo beneath me.

"Now." She tugs at my shirt, leading me toward the pantry. With dopey hearts in my eyes, I follow her through the door, leaving any thought of Solomon asleep on the couch behind. Though it's filled with various foods, boxes, and baking items, the pantry is spacious enough I can pin Andi against the shelving to devour her mouth.

"The bed is too big without you in it," she says, skimming cool fingertips along my obliques. I jerk at the ticklish sensation, and she travels to my waistband, finding me hard for her.

"I'm sorry, babygirl." I seal my mouth over hers, groaning when she pumps me twice. Her ass fits perfectly in my grip, and I squeeze her to remind her of our time in the basement. "Let me make it up to you."

"We don't have that kind of time."

My needy girl.

I spin her around, wincing as she releases my waistband and it snaps against my cock. I place her hands on the shelving and slide my own into the front of her pants, finding her bare and already wet when I glide my fingers over her clit. She mewls when I circle the needy bud, dipping my fingers lower to gather some of her arousal.

"Quiet, Dandi." I nip at her ear. "Or else you'll wake your brother and get my ass kicked before we even get to the good part."

She slumps against my shoulder as I massage her clit in circles, spreading her legs with my feet as I explore her warmth. I brush that spot inside her that makes her whimper, and her hand clamps around mine to hold me there.

"Oh, god. Don't stop," she pants, and my cock weeps at the pleading tone in her voice.

I need to be inside her right now.

A few more circles and she explodes beneath me, somehow managing to keep quiet as her body jolts through an orgasm. My sweats hit the ground, and she lifts her leg onto a shelf, making it easy to slide into her. The moment my tip touches that same spot inside her, Andi moans loudly, thrusting her hips back.

"Faster," she says.

I continue at a maddeningly slow pace as I look for something to muffle her cries. The way I want—need—her, there's no way she can stay quiet enough not to rouse her brother. My gaze lands on the perfect remedy, and I snatch it quickly and place it in front of her.

"Bite down on this." I slide the lemon into her mouth and lift her leg one shelf higher. "Touch yourself, babygirl."

She doesn't waste any time moving her fingers to her clit, and I grip her waist, giving free rein to my baser instincts. Trying to be quiet while having sex in a pantry is probably just as difficult as it is trying to tiptoe out of a toddler's room, but we do a damn good job of finding a rhythm. Moments pass in a haze of grunts and kisses, nips and licks, and just as my orgasm barrels toward me, Andi comes apart at the seams. Lemon juice spews from the peel, dripping down her neck as she rides out her orgasm with a sour face, and I follow her down the spiral, coming so hard I see stars.

I slide her pants back up, kissing her thighs, waist, and then her neck. "Mmm, sticky," I say, drawing her bottom lip between my teeth and cupping her dripping pussy through the fabric. "Just the way I like you."

She laughs and bumps me back with her ass. Once we're sorted, I peek out the door, ensuring the kitchen is clear before we both exit. Andi sits at the table while I grab some glasses from the cabinet.

A crash inside the pantry startles me, and I drop the cups in the sink with a clatter. Solomon rushes in from the living room, sleepy-eyed yet ready to fight.

"What happened?" he asks, blinking through the haze of sleep. "Everyone okay?"

I sputter, trying to find words that refuse to form as Andi moves toward the pantry and opens the door. Cans spill out onto the floor, and the shelf I just had Andi propped up on is hanging off the wall.

My face burns and a tingle inside my chest tells me I'm not breathing. I suck in a sharp breath and fight the urge to flee the scene as Solo says, "That scared the shit out of me."

"I hope you didn't piss on the couch like a little baby," Andi replies, breaking the tension. My mom comes out to check on things, and even though she shares a look with me that tells me she knows exactly what happened to that shelf, she doesn't say a word. Thankfully, Solo doesn't comment on why both of us were in the kitchen as we clean up.

Andi takes her glass of water to the bedroom, and I slyly wink at her before she disappears into the hallway. Solo and I settle back into the living room, but my racing thoughts still charge forth. I want to come clean to Solo right now, to tell him I love his sister and want to be with her, but I won't cross that boundary until Andi tells me she's ready.

"I missed my wingman last night." Solomon stares the ceiling, though I catch his gaze dart to me. I give him a half-hearted acknowledgment, but I can tell he's ruminating on something. It doesn't take long for him to finally ask, "Hey, how'd you end up running into Andi yesterday?"

Though I could feel the question coming, my stomach still flips. I slide my sweaty palms along the cover, lungs deflating as I release a calming breath. "Mom ordered a cake and needed me to pick it up. I didn't know Andi was back in town, or else I wouldn't have gone there."

"I didn't know she was coming back either," he says, eyebrows bunched and a slight frown on his face. "I'm honestly surprised she even got into your car. Last time I checked, she had your picture up on a wall, complete with devil horns and a tail."

I chuckle at that. "You're as surprised as I am."

When he's silent for too long, I almost think he's fallen asleep.

"Thanks for looking out for her." He blows out a breath. "She probably would've hitchhiked and been picked up by a serial killer or something." I start to respond that it wasn't that big of a deal when he adds, "At least it was you and not someone who was going to take advantage of her."

His words deliver a blow straight to my conscience. While things between me and Andi have changed, they started out because I needed her to lie for me. I took advantage of her situation to bolster mine with Nana.

"Solo..." The words bubble to the surface, the truth burning my core.

"Nah, man, seriously," he cuts in. "I really appreciate you taking care of her. I know you had plans for finding a bar bunny yesterday and the last thing you wanted to do was tote around my kid sister, but I'm sure there will be some ladies looking for a bad boy tomorrow night too." He laughs it off, but it's another bomb set off inside my mind. I'll always be 'the bad boy' to Solomon, the man only worried about a warm body beneath him and his win/loss rate.

Maybe Nana was right in forcing me to find someone to settle down with, but in Solomon's mind, Andi is off limits. A coldness settles in my bones. Come tomorrow, a line will be drawn in the sand.

Either I lose my best friend or the woman I'm in love with.

Chapter Fifteen
Andi

Win's hunched shoulders tells me he's on edge the moment I walk into the kitchen. An uneasiness settles into my core as I watch his finger round the rim of a steaming mug, not acknowledging my presence outside of a nod.

"Good morning?" I ask, arching a brow to Win's mom doing a crossword at the island. She shrugs as if to say 'I don't know', and worry swells inside my stomach.

"Morning," he says, not looking up from his cup.

I blink a few times, unsure if I'm dreaming this weird interaction. After last night, I thought we were on good footing. We made it through the evening without Solomon or Nana catching onto us, and we got to spend one more night in each other's arms.

Solomon enters the kitchen, stretching and releasing a loud groan. "Morning everyone." He claps Win on the shoulder, staring out the window at the glistening snow. "Looks like the storm is over."

"Yup," Win replies.

His one word answers send my mind on a chase of memories to see what happened between last night and this morning. Did I do something? Was he mad I didn't tell Solo about us last night after everything happened?

Yeah, that's probably it. Maybe he's sick of pretending in front of everyone and wants me to tell him it's okay? I'm not sure that I'm ready today. I know I'll get there, but, with how this morning has started off, it's for the best that I leave before things get more tense.

"I should get going," I say to no one in particular. I retreat to the basement to grab the gnomes I whittled yesterday and clean up any tools I used. The door opens and shuts, and Win appears at the bottom of the stairs.

"What's wrong?" I ask.

He tormented gaze lands everywhere but on me. "I'm sorry."

"Sorry for what?" He stares at his shoes, rubbing the back of his neck. He's gone into safe mode and closed himself off from me. "I'm sorry I dragged you into this. I should've answered his call earlier."

"Dragged me into this?" I scoff, hurt spearing my heart. "You didn't drag me into anything, Win. The past two nights were...well, it changed things."

"I'll still help you with your landlord, and I'll tell Nana the truth," he says to the floor.

"No, Win. What are you even talking about?" Fire kindles in my stomach. His change of heart makes absolutely no sense. "Why would you do that?"

Sorrowful eyes meet mine, and it sends a pang through my heart. I can tell from the set to his jaw that his mind is made up. "We made a deal, and I'll honor that."

Fury pours into my veins. "Fuck that. You don't get to do this, Win."

He tugs at the strands of his beard. "Do what, Andi? This can't go on."

"Why not?" I ask, an air of pleading to my tone. "What even is *this*?" I gesture between us. "Cuz it's not just fucking, Win. What happened last night?" His entire body inflates with his deep breath, but when he looks at me, all I can see is the weariness in his slumped posture. "You can't brush this off like it was nothing to you. Like *I'm* nothing to you."

In a swift motion, my chin is in between his thumb and forefinger. "You are *everything* to me, Andi." His gravelly tone busts through the dam of emotions I've built. "I wish things could be different, but I won't tarnish you again to elevate my own standing."

"Stop being scared about what everyone else thinks." I swat him away and forcefully poke my finger into his pec. I'm well aware of the hypocrisy of my statement, but I woke up this morning with a clarity I haven't had in awhile. I'd rather be happy and have Win in my life than to be miserable and still have my family. "Fight for us."

His lips crash into mine, arms wrapping around me in a tight embrace. The kiss is all passion and fire, a game of tag as our tongues chase each other across the rift I can feel opening between us. He breathes, and I inhale that breath and store it away in my lungs as he breaks the kiss, unlatching himself from me.

"I can't." With a look of defeat he disappears up the steps.

Barbed wire wraps itself around my heart, puncturing the stupid organ every time it deigns to thump. I thought things would be different this time around, that we'd both grown enough to finally see that we belong together. But I guess I'm not the only one too scared of what everyone will think to step out of my comfort zone.

He told you not to fall in love with him.

God, how did he manage to make me fall again in only forty-eight hours? Did I ever really stop?

Tears blur my vision as I stand alone in the basement, fuming about his cowardice. After the bonfire incident, he went off the deep end and got sent to juvie, and I was the one who had to deal with the aftermath of not only being embarrassed in front of the entire school, but also being shipped off to live with my aunt as if I'd tarnished the family name.

I forgave him for that. I foolishly believed there was something deeper between us, that we could reconcile the past with the present because our chemistry was still there. It never changed, and my care for him never wavered.

Hearing Win talk about tarnishing me further drives a wooden stake of betrayal into my heart. I let him walk away from me years ago because I was angry and afraid of what my parents and classmates thought, but I'm sick of letting what others think I should do direct my actions.

I deserve to be happy and thriving, unafraid that I'm not living up to someone else's dreams for me. It's time I let go of the chains binding me to what others say I should do and start living my life the way I want to.

And that begins with showing the man I still love that he's not getting rid of me that easily.

Chapter Sixteen
Win

My feet are like cinder blocks as I trudge to the kitchen with a sinking feeling in my stomach. Andi's stricken face haunts me, the way the light slowly ebbed from her bright eyes when I told her I wouldn't allow her reputation to suffer again because of me.

"Where'd you go?" Solomon asks, leaning on his elbows.

My mom's heated gaze is a brand on my cheek as I make coffee, but I can't bear to look at her. To see the disappointment etched into her features. Forcing a smile, I greet Nana and sit on the stool in front of my best friend.

"To hell," I reply. "Had to renew my yearly membership."

He snorts into his drink. "Funny, funny. Where's Andi?"

Swallowing swords would be easier than answering that question, but I somehow manage to say, "Probably gathering her stuff to leave."

"She's leaving?" Nana perks up. "Not until she eats breakfast. Don't you let her leave without feeding the girl, Winchester."

The condemnation in my grandmother's voice is similar to her closing arguments; direct, cutting, and leaves you lambasted in front of your peers. I don't want Andi to leave either, but I know she can't stay. The decision to trick Nana was my half-baked idea—an idea I don't regret because it gave me time with Andi—so I have to deal with the impending fall out.

Solomon stares at the collar of my shirt. I flinch and reach for my neck, rubbing it to feel what captured his attention. I recall Andi sucking hard on the skin, her fingers digging into my traps when she came apart beneath me. My stomach pitches and churns, and I shift uncomfortably under his scrutiny.

Why didn't I just make up an excuse to why he couldn't come inside?

"Ginger missed you the other night." He crosses his arms and juts his chin. "The ladies wondered why you weren't there."

Heat from the ceramic coffee cup warms my hands as I twist it around in my palms, unable to look at my best friend. If I opened my mouth right now, I'm not sure what would come out. I slept with your sister? I'm still in love with her, but I asked her to pretend to be my girlfriend so Nana would retire and make me a partner?

Because I value my nose in its current position, I utter none of those statements. Instead, I gulp down coffee and offer a small nod.

"I'm sure they'll get over it," Nana chimes in. "Andi's perfect for him."

I choke on my coffee, spewing droplets all over the table. A firm smack to the back helps clear the remnants of the scorching hot liquid. I pat my shirt down with a napkin, desperately trying to come up with an excuse for what Nana said. No sooner does my gaze meet Solomon's drawn together eyebrows, than Andi bounds into the room, a smile on her face as she nears me.

"Sorry, I'm late," she says, brushing rogue wispy brown curls behind her ears. "Got caught up in the workshop."

Andi stops at the table as I'm still in the process of catching my breath, leaning forward in slow motion. I realize what's happening a split second before her lips meet mine. A primal urge to deepen the kiss slinks down my spine, but a loud screech nixes the thought.

My eyes pop open to find Solo staring at us with his mouth agape. I break the kiss, pushing back from Andi as if that will somehow reverse what just happened. Solo stands, rapidly blinking as if he's processing the moment.

"What the fuck, dude?" he yells, arms thrown in offense.

"Language, boy," Nana chides.

"That's my sister." He points at Andi as if I don't know who he's speaking about. "No. Just no."

"It's not what you think," I say. *But it is, isn't it?*

Andi scoffs.

My neck is stiff as I clock the look of confusion on everyone's faces—except Andi's. Her eyes are two fireballs ready to take aim and fire at me. I should've pulled Solo outside to tell him what was going on.

Which is what? That you respect the hell out of him but you're in love with his sister, or that you're a dumbass who lied to your Nana and begged Andi to pretend to love you.

Fuck, I'm all over the place. But after everything that happened between me and Andi, I can't tell another lie. And I've already told too many lies—at this point I'm committing perjury on the stand of real life.

Solo's fists clench and unclench, his face slowly turning a shade of red I've seen too often when he's primed for a fight. "Someone better start talking."

"It's pretty obvious, isn't it?" Andi replies, moving to my side and lacing our fingers.

Is she trying to keep up the ruse because Nana is here? The action draws his attention, and a sneer forms on his face before his glare snaps to me, betrayal pouring out in the tight wrinkles at his temples.

"What are y'all yappin' about?" Nana asks, head on a swivel.

"Solo—" I start before he cuts me off.

"Save it man." He scoffs and turns to Andi. "I thought you were smarter than that."

"Don't talk to her like that," I retort.

Andi crosses her arms. "What's that supposed to mean?"

Solo rounds the table toward his sister. Even though I know he'd never hurt her, instincts kick in, and I pull her toward me. He doesn't miss the gesture. His nostrils flare under his unblinking stare, and he bares his teeth.

"What is this?" He motions between us. "Some bad boy bucket list, Andi?"

His words strike that familiar chord in my chest, the one that reminds me I'll never shake that persona placed on me years ago. "Leave it alone, Solo."

"Screw you, Win. I *knew* something was weird about last night. I can't believe you'd do something like this...again." He stumbles on the word as if emotion has him in its clutches. With a heavy sigh, his gaze settles back on Andi, whose face is the picture of calm. "Did you know he was supposed to meet me the other night at the bar?" I can tell where he's going with his message, but I'm helpless to stop it. This is all my fault. And I'll have to deal with the consequences. He doesn't give her a moment to answer before he continues, "He wanted to go prowling for a chick to pretend to be his girlfriend."

The Jenga blocks of my life tumble down, crashing against the tile with a loud clang. Soft footsteps retreat from the room, and in my peripheral, I catch my mom's disappointed expression as she follows Nana.

"Yes," Andi replies. "I knew that. But—"

"And you're still dumb enough to let him get in your pants?" he yells. "He leaves the bar with at least three numbers every single time we go."

I recoil at his words. Yes, women give me their number every time I go to the bar, but I've never gone home with any of them. I don't sleep around. I never have. And I've certainly never given my heart to anyone but the woman who stole it years ago.

I never cared about Solomon's opinion of me because I didn't think I'd ever have a chance with Andi again, but hearing the way he views me—his supposed best friend—hurts more than I expected.

"Stop yelling at her," I reply, anger seeping into my tone. "It's not her fault."

"Win, no." Andi grasps my arm.

"I trusted you." His stare is cold enough to give me frostbite. "You hurt her once before, and I forgave you then, but I can't stand by and let you do it again."

All the fight drains out of me, and I can't bear to look at Andi, to see the pain of those memories flashing across her face. I'm frozen, my anger doused by the damning truth in his words.

"Whoa." Andi steps between us, pushing against our chests with force to break us apart. She spins on her heels, ire coating her tone. "I am a grown ass woman, Solomon. I don't need you to be my knight in shining armor, especially since you never came to my defense years ago when dad and mom sent me away." She sips in a quick breath. "I can make my own decisions about my life."

"He's not good enough for you," Solomon says, spearing my already tattered heart. He's not saying anything I don't already know, but hearing it driven home again and again from someone I thought saw the true me, defeats me in a way I can't put into words. "He's just using you to get ahead."

"You don't know him as well as you think you do then." Her gaze settles on me, eyebrows squished together. "Would you say something,

Win?" Her voice breaks in a desperate plea. "Tell him that's not what this is."

Words take shape, readying themselves to launch off my tongue. My mouth opens, and nothing comes out but a resigned sigh. Solomon is right. While I wasn't expecting things to happen between me and Andi, I went into this *using* her. Getting my promotion was the only thing that mattered, and if I hadn't run into Andi at the bakery, I would've convinced someone else to help me.

It doesn't matter that we made a mutually beneficial deal. Once things crossed from professional to personal, we should've stopped and had a conversation. I never want Andi to feel like I only wanted her because of what she could offer me, the benefit to my career. My dad was a user that didn't care how he hurt people, and that's the last thing I want to be.

Pushing her away is the only way I know how to keep her from continuing to be hurt by my poor decisions.

"He's right," I choke out.

"What?" Andi squeaks.

Pain lances through me as I stare at her wet lashes, fanned out over expressive brown eyes. "I shouldn't have let you pretend we were dating. It was wrong to lie about it to Nana, and I'm sorry I dragged you into this. It was selfish of me to use you for my own benefit." She reaches for me, but I back away. "You deserve the world."

Regret wells up beneath my ribcage, and I struggle to catch a breath past the painful jabs I've just given my heart. If I don't get out of here now, I'll take back everything I just said. My vision blurs as I stumble to the front door and fling it open, light blinding me. Snow smacks my face as the biting wind whips around me, but I can barely feel it over the pounding in my skull.

Part of me wants to run back inside and tell Andi she's right, that there's more to us than just this deal, but it wouldn't be fair to her. She deserves so much more than a life with the town fuck-up.

Chapter Seventeen

The slam of the door continues to ring inside my ears the entire way back to Win's room where I gather my clothes and purse in a daze. He didn't fight for us—for me.

Solomon stands in the doorway, his posture rigid. I dig my fingers into my palms but keep my chin high, fury washing over me at his smirk. He ruined every good thing about the past two days—made it seem like Win was still that immature, teenaged kid—and Win let him.

"I'm just trying to help you, Andi," he sighs, crossing his arms.

I scoff and blow out an exasperated breath. "Don't kid yourself, Solo. You haven't done anything to help me in the last ten years, so why start now?"

He steps into the room, looking over his shoulder as if Win's going to attack. "He's not right for you, Andi."

Anger bubbles to the surface, and I push him back, steel lacing my spine. "What makes you think you know what's right for me? You don't even *know* me anymore. You've been so caught up in your own life, impressing mom and dad with your business ventures that you forgot about the sister they shipped away."

He blinks as if the rose colored glasses he views his life through have finally broken and his mouth opens like a fish taking its last breath. "I—"

"Save it, Solo. I don't need your excuses about why you didn't call or why you don't come to see me. Just like our parents, you're too worried about your image to care about anyone else."

"That's not true," he replies, crossing his arms.

"It's not?" I release a self-deprecating laugh. "When was the last time you called me? Do you even know my address if you wanted to come visit? What about my career? Do you know what I do?" I wait a beat, watching for any hint of clarity. "Let me save you the trouble. You know nothing about what I do or want. But guess who does?"

He snarls. "So, he's kept this...relationship from me for years?"

I sigh and exhale a deep breath. "No, asswipe. It took him all of four hours to learn that information because *he* cares. He always has. What does it say about you that the person you say isn't good enough for me, knows more about me and my hope and dreams?"

"A lot, I guess." He rubs the back of his neck, toeing the carpet with his sneakers. "But he hurt you."

"That was ten years ago, and we both hurt each other. It's *you* who hasn't gotten over the past." I sigh, stepping closer to him and forcing him to look at me. "Win might've hurt my feelings with some words that stung, but you hurt my heart. You know how mom and dad are, yet you told them about what happened when I asked you not to, *you* got me sent away and then cast me aside just like they did. It was more important for you to be the apple of their eye than for you to be a good big brother."

"That's not—that's not true. I never meant to tell them." His mask of betrayal slips from his face. "I was so angry when I heard what happened that the words spilled out. I didn't mean for you to get sent away."

I shrug, indignant. "Well, your actions caused just as much damage as his words. And thus far, he's the only one that's apologized."

"You're right. I've been a shit brother." The tension releases from his jaw, and he folds in on himself. "I'm sorry. I thought I was protecting you by keeping their focus on me."

I'm speechless, unsure how to respond now that his bravado of a protective older brother has deflated.

"What's that supposed to mean?"

He shrugs. "You've always marched to the beat of your own drum, and I've always envied that. I think *they* envy that. That they can't control you the way they do to me. I'm trapped. All of my business partners in some way, shape, or form, are friends with Dad. I can't tell them to shove it or not show up to Sunday dinners like you can."

For so long we've been on opposite sides, not understanding what the other was going through. I always felt like he delighted in their adoration and attention but hearing him talk about feeling trapped spears my heart. Parental expectations suck. Maybe I'm lucky because they see me as a black sheep when his perceived disobedience can have real life ramifications.

"Our parents suck." I sigh, looking back at the bed where Win and I finally made our peace.

"Yes, they do. But it doesn't change the fact that he used you to lie to his Nana so he could get a promotion."

"With my consent." Annoyed he's not letting this go, I say, "Did you ever stop to think about what *I* was getting out of this deal?"

He winces sheepishly. "No?"

"The guy I rented my carpentry shop from evicted me without reason and took my deposit. We made a deal that he'd help me with my sleazy landlord, and I'd help convince his Nana that he was serious about something more than just his career..."

"I'm sensing a but," he says.

I shrug. "Old feelings came back. Well, I guess they never really left." Solo exhales, but I charge on, determined to make him see this from my point of view. "We never really got closure on what happened between us, seeing as he ended up in juvie and I got shipped off to Aunt Marysa's house."

He nods as I sling my purse over my shoulder, following me out of Win's room. "I get that. But do you really think this is a good idea? I mean, he's my best friend...and you're my sister. It was weird back then, and then I lost both of you. I don't want that to happen again."

"It's not about you," I chide, stopping outside of the kitchen when I hear Nana and Win's mom talking. I turn to Solomon and say, "Win isn't the same kid he was back then. He grew up into a smart, ambitious, and loyal man determined to achieve his dreams, even though he had a rough past. You're still too stuck on who he was to see who he's become." Even though we've made headway in this conversation, anger simmers beneath my skin at the turn of events. "And now you've made him feel like he isn't good enough for me, and he believed you."

"You're right, again." He gives me a crooked smile, bumping into my shoulder as if we're teenagers again. "I'm sorry," he sighs. "I'll find him and talk to him."

"You better, or I'll castrate you." I point my thumb over my shoulder, signifying I'm going to talk to the women currently watching our inter- action at the island. "I'll catch up with you later."

He gives me a side hug and disappears through the front door. My feet squeak on the tile floor as I face the matriarch firing squad. Somehow, I manage to meet their gaze instead of avoiding it. What I did was wrong, there's no point in pretending like the cards aren't all face up on the table.

"That was interesting," Win's mom says.

I chuckle nervously, inching my way closer to the island. "I'm sorry about all this. It spiraled into something bigger than it should've been."

"You can say that again." Nana playfully scoffs, relaxing into her seat.

"I'm truly sorry," I babble, digging my toes into the soles of my shoes. "Please, don't be mad at Win. He just wanted to make you proud and show you that it's okay to retire because the firm would be in good hands."

"I'm not angry, sweetie." The warmth in her tone feels like forgiveness instead of condemnation. "And don't you be mad at him for being a simpleton. It's clear as day he still loves you, regardless of what the dumb-dumb said earlier."

I paste on a weak smile and beg the tears not to fall and betray my hopefulness at her statement. As much as I want to believe everything will work out, I don't know that Win is ready to put the past behind him when he still truly believes he's not good enough for me or that he's tarnishing my reputation. Sure, it didn't help that my brother decided to drive that notion back into his mind, but all the good he's done as a lawyer is proof enough that he's not the same person anymore.

"I hope it all works out for the best. I'm so sorry everything was ruined." I turn to Win's mom, Holly. "Thank you for having me, I think it's probably best I leave and let you guys sort things out."

Holly wraps me in a hug, pressing a kiss to my hair. "He'll come around. It's always been you," she whispers.

A sense of calm washes over me. "I hope so."

Chapter Eighteen
Win

Frigid air burns my lungs when I inhale deeply, searing through the emotions I've been walking around for twenty minutes trying to expel. My fingertips are numb, and the bare skin on my arms is on fire because in my haste I forgot a coat. Ignoring the chill in my bones, I shuffle along the sidewalk, being mindful of any patches of ice.

Shame is a shadow, following closely behind me no matter where I turn, illuminating the ways in which I've failed not only Andi and Nana, but myself. I've spent my entire adulthood shedding the shackles of my past, hoping people will see the good I've done and look at me as someone deserving of everything I have. My record might've been sealed as a kid, but the memory of the burning bridge still lives on in the minds of the people it affected, and it's their frowns and whispers that follow me as I run from the one person I want to deserve, chased away by her brother—my best friend.

The crisp, earthy smell of day-old snow calms me until an engine rumbles at my back, my favorite hip-hop song thumping from the speakers. I don't even have to glance over my shoulder to know who it is. As if my thoughts summoned him, Solo pulls up beside me and rolls down his window.

"It's a bit cold to be walking around without a jacket on, don't cha think?"

I tighten my arms around my body and continue walking. Why does he care when he just made it clear our friendship is over? "I'm fine."

His brakes squeal as he veers into a parking lot, leaving fresh tire tracks in the snow. I startle at his slammed door, but I press forward, trying to gather my scattered thoughts and warm my numb fingers in case he's primed for a fight.

The last thing I want to do is brawl with my best friend because I slept with his sister again, but if that's what he wants, I'm ready.

Knuckles slam against my face, making stars appear in my eyes.

Okay, maybe I wasn't as ready as I thought.

I get my bearings and spin with my fists raised to find Solo with his hands up in surrender, smirking as he walks toward me. "You deserved that. Bro code was broken."

Pain blooms in my jaw, and I massage it out, fighting the urge to clock him one back. He's right. I broke bro code. Hell, I broke it multiple times, and I can't say that I wouldn't do it again just to feel what it'd be like if Andi was truly mine.

"Sorry, man." A puff of white cloud leaves my mouth with my heavy sigh. "I know I royally fucked things up, and I get it if you don't wanna be friends anymore, but—"

"What are we? Twelve?" He scoffs, raising his fists again. A flash of the old Solomon, the one I used to tousle with after school appears a moment before he puts on a pretend angry face. "Fight me."

Goosebumps skitter over my skin, brought on by adrenaline and a cold snap of wind. The difference in his demeanor from the house to standing in front of me is jarring, but I figure if this is his way of working through what happened between us—and hopefully moving on—then I'll play along. "Fight you? You want your ass kicked that badly?"

"What I want is..." He feigns a jab but plows me in the side with a hook. Air rushes out of me, and I stifle a groan as I return his punch with my own, fist landing in his solar plexus. "For you to apologize to my sister for not fighting for her...again."

"What?" His words stun me, and adding insult to injury, he takes the opportunity lightly slap my face. "Did you not hear anything that was said inside?"

We circle each other, and out of the corner of my eye I see a neighbor peering out of her curtains. She's probably wondering what two grown men are doing fighting each other in the middle of a snowstorm, but weirder things have happened on the streets of Boston. Solo roundhouse kicks my butt, and I nearly slip on a patch of ice at the edge of the sidewalk.

"What are you, the Karate Kid?" I ask.

"I heard everything you said inside." He pauses in thought, giving me a moment to capitalize on his distraction. Lunging forward, I wrap an arm around his neck and pull him into a chokehold. He grunts, tugging on my arms for a sip of air. "And I listened to everything she said once you left."

My grip on him loosens, and like the asshole he is, he swoops under me, grabbing my leg and heaving his back under my stomach as he lifts and slams me on the firmly packed snow, knocking the wind from my lungs. His words clang around my mind as I blink away the pain developing at the back of my skull.

"What did she say?" The question leaks out of me in a whisper as my lungs fight to expand correctly.

I squint at Solo's silhouette blocking out the sun. He's bent over, perched on his knees, sucking in small breaths. He flashes me a remorseful smile. "She called me out on being a shit brother and not defending her in school, and basically told me I was being a dick to you and needed to fix it or she'd make sure I never have kids."

Laughing hurts my ribs, but I can't help it. That woman's fascination with castration should worry me, but all it does is remind me of her lips wrapped around said appendage. Solo extends offers to help me up, and I eye him suspiciously but figure he's not going to kick me while I'm down.

"There's nothing to fix." My eyes grow hot, prickling with emotions I push deep down. "She gave me another chance to show her what she means to me, and my dumbass let her down like the fuck up I am."

I flinch when he clamps down on my shoulder. "And that right there is exactly why you *do* deserve her."

"Huh?" I do a double take as a sudden rush of cold settles in my bones. Did I give him brain damage with that headlock?

My brows raise to my hairline when he nods over to his car. "Come on, let's get warm and talk."

Unsure if I'm being led to my death, I slowly follow, shivering through the brutal wind. Thankfully, the seats are still warm when I enter the car.

He lowers the volume on the radio, turning to me with a serious expression. "I owe you an apology."

Baffled by his sudden admission, I say, "What do you mean?"

"I've been a shit friend to you." He stares out the front windshield where the snow quickly gathers. "You got handed a rep in school because of your father, then after you burned the bridge leading to the mayor's house—"

"—I didn't know it was the mayor's house, and it was an accident." My face heats, embarrassed at all the chaos I caused. "It was just my shit luck that it was strike three after getting scooped up by the cops for that weed."

He ignores my interjection and continues, "—you got sent to juvie and it perpetuated the persona. When we started hanging out, I kinda got used to you being the 'bad boy' to my 'good guy' routine. It worked for us—for me—picking up girls. I didn't think about how it made you feel to still be looked at as *that* guy. I know you're not the same dude you were back in school, but I kept reminding you of it without thinking how it would affect how you thought about yourself."

Slack-jawed, I stare at him, surprised at the depth of his thoughts. Solomon's never been introspective, preferring to keep things light and humorous, but his slumped shoulders and heartfelt apology show me he's serious.

"Thanks, man," I breathe out, brain void of more words.

"I've been selfish, only worried about myself for so long that I didn't see I was hurting you and my sister. Andi was in trouble, and she didn't tell me. She told you, and you found a way to be there for her, even after all that happened between you guys." He scoffs as if he can't quite believe what he's saying. "I thought she still hated you, but I was wrong."

His words fill me with something akin to hope. I want to hear the truth in them, that Andi could feel something more than just attraction to me, but my brain won't let me.

"She probably still does." I scrape along my beard, wincing at the bruise I already feel blooming. "Sex doesn't change what the heart feels."

"Eww, gross, dude." Solomon pushes me against the window and pretends to barf. "But seriously, man." He shivers, pulling a disgusted face. "Sex might not change what the heart feels, but it can amplify what's been hidden for ten years. Do you still love her?"

"I never stopped." I let those words hang in the air, filling the car with the truth of that statement. "It's only ever been her. But I never thought she'd forgive me—that I deserved her forgiveness—and I've been so focused on my career and proving to everyone else that I've changed that any relationships fell by the wayside."

"You gotta stop being afraid of what people will think of you. You know who you are now, and so does Andi. I'm sorry my dumbass comments made you feel like you needed to be a certain way."

I never looked at it as being afraid of what others thought of me but as a sign that I was undeserving of things because of my past. But he's right, I need to stop allowing what others think of the person I used to be and focus on the man I am now. And that man is deserving of love. Particularly one fiery, gnome carpenter's love.

"Damn, man." I lean back in the seat and cross my arms over my aching ribs. My muscle twinges and my body is fatigued "You're right. But did you need to lay me out to say all that?"

"Had to take the opportunity when you were distracted to finally get a win over you." He chuckles, sliding the gear shift into drive and pulling out onto the empty street. "Plus, I needed to be certain you're serious about her. She deals with enough disappointment from our parents. I didn't want her to get her hopes up."

I nod, understanding where he's coming from. "She's it, man."

Five minutes later, he pulls up in front of my mom's house. He rolls down his window, yelling to me as I approach the steps, "Don't fuck it up."

He doesn't wait for me to answer before he drives away. I take a moment to think about what I'm going to say to convince Andi we need to give this a fair shot. Warmth and laughter greet me as I enter the house in search of the woman I love. A stop in the kitchen reveals Mom and Nana at the table.

"Where is she?" I ask, searching the room as if she's hiding.

My mom's pained look tell me a split second before Nana says, "She left."

I stare at my feet, my body sagging in defeat. I'm too late. I pushed her away, told her that she deserved better than what I could give her—the words of a fearful boy—and then I went and proved it by leaving, by walking away and not fighting for her again.

My head spins and my body throbs as if pain is the least I deserve for being a dumbass. The sound of a chair scraping against the floor draws my attention to where my mom is getting up from the table.

"I'll let you guys talk." She carries her plate to the island, gulping down the last dregs of wine before leaving the room.

Nana nods to the seat across the table. "Sit."

Her stern look makes my armpits sweat and my stomach churn. I don't know how much of the spat between me, Andi, and Solo she heard, but my heart palpates knowing I have to come clean about my deceit.

Shuffling over to the seat, I sigh. "I'm sorry, Nana."

"For what?" She rasps.

I lean back, wincing as the chair spindle meets with the spot I'm sure is already bruised from Solomon's punches. "I messed up and betrayed your trust. I was so worried about showing you I had something other than the job that I convinced Andi to pretend to be my girlfriend."

I freeze at her smoky laugh. She reaches across the table, her wrinkled skin cool against mine despite being wrapped around a warm mug.

"You thought after fifty years of being a lawyer that I couldn't tell when my own grandson was telling a fib?" My mouth pops open, and I have the urge to slide beneath the table to cover my heated face. She knew the entire time that I was lying, yet she still told me not to let Andi get away again. Even she saw there was something more between us than just this stupid deal we made.

"I'm sorry," I repeat, unsure of what I can do to make things right. She doesn't seem all that upset about what happened, but she's basically a safe when it comes to emotions.

"Would you stop apologizing?" she chides, releasing my hand. "I didn't get to where I'm at by letting little white lies upset me. Your grandfather was the best lawyer I knew, and he helped me see through to the intent of why people do and say certain things. I knew why you lied to me about Andi, but I could also see how smitten you genuinely were with her."

Her smile makes my heart wither. She should be angry or disappointed that I lied to her, but she's sitting here unbothered.

"I put a lot of pressure on you to settle down, but I want you to have something—someone—to come home to. This job can suck the life out of you, and you'll need someone that is ready to pour love into you at the end of the day. Your gramps was that for me, and I for him. From what I saw in just two days, Andi did that for you."

"She's..." I inhale a deep breath, smiling as I think back on the last two days. Ten years didn't erase the feelings. They hid in the deep, dark cave of my heart just waiting for the day she'd waltz back in with a flashlight and a broom to sweep off the cobwebs. "Everything."

"I know, son. Anyone within a mile of you guys can tell you're it for each other. Stop worrying about what all them old farts at the firm think about you. You'll be made a partner, not because you're my grandson but because you're the best option for ushering the firm into the next century."

"Really?"

She sighs deeply. "I should smack you upside the head for making me spell it out for you. You have the highest number of cases closed, you've brought more clients to the firm than at least three others combined, you're able to handle a large case load, and even though your average fees aren't as high as some of the others, you manage to bring in more money than them."

I turn away from her penetrating gaze, and blink away tears threatening to fall. Her words refuse to settle in my mind. Even after I lied to her, she still believes I can be successful and continue the family legacy.

It's only you who believed you couldn't do it.

My lungs fill with a deep, satisfying breath. "Thank you so much, Nana. I can't tell you how much it means to me that you trust me with the firm. I'll make you proud."

"I have no doubt about it." She scowls. "But if you lie to me again, I'll kick your scrawny ass."

Her comment about lying prickles something at the back of my mind. I squint back at her, rolling a thought around inside my mind. "Nana?"

"Yes?"

"If you were going to make me a partner anyway, why did you say I needed to have a serious girlfriend?"

She relaxes into the chair and chuckles. "I'm getting old, boy. I want great-grandbabies." I burst out laughing, and she leans over. "Now go get your girl back."

Chapter Nineteen
Andi

Cool air follows me into Grams's bakery, chilling my ankles and bringing along the loamy scent of soil and fresh pine. Outside, a plump Santa rings his bells, asking for donations for the local children's charity from two older gentlemen. They drop a handful of change in the red bucket and come inside.

It's been two days since I caught an Uber from Win's house. After the fiasco with my brother and Nana, Win blew up my phone with texts when he realized I left. I didn't even check what he had to say. I needed space to breathe, and to figure out how I felt about the entire situation. For all I know, those messages still sitting unopened could be him saying that the entire thing was mistake, and he wants to forget it, but I've yet to find the courage to find out.

"We'll have two cranberry orange scones, please," a man says, wrapping his plaid scarf tighter to his neck. "And a slice of that tuxedo cake, if you don't mind."

Boxing up their order, I wonder if I'm just prolonging the hurt and confusion. Had he stayed instead of walking out, we wouldn't be in this situation. Or at least I hope we wouldn't be. Solomon fixed my car, and let me know they worked things out, but he didn't tell me how or what they spoke about. I'm in the dark on what's coming until I read those messages, and the fear of being shut down again scares me.

"You tell your grandmother we'll be ordering a cake for the nursing home Christmas party soon. She always makes the best angel food cake," the other man says as they pay and leave.

I smile and relax against the counter. A newspaper peeks out from where I threw my purse on the shelf below, and the highlighted rentals draw my attention. Win said he'd still represent me in the case against my landlord, but I don't know if it's a good idea with everything that happened to continue using him, even though I kept up my end of the deal.

My shop is on a temporary hiatus until I can make my gnomes and get them out in a timely manner, and that feels like another failure. My dad's voice echoes in my mind, reminding me that carpentry isn't going to pay the bills—that dreams and passions aren't what puts food on the table and that I should have a man to take care of me.

This setback feels like I'm proving him right.

But there's an even louder voice telling me there was a man who believed in me, one that made sure I had everything I needed to get back on track and get some of my orders complete. Win didn't have to let me use the woodshop in the basement—he didn't even have to tell me about it—but he believes in my abilities. He bought my gnomes without knowing they were mine, and that makes me giddier than a little kid hopped up on sugary treats after they sneak into Santa's workshop.

His faith in me spurs me on. In spite of my parents' doubts and lack of love and attention, I'm determined to make this into a viable career, one where I'm fulfilled and happy. I scan the highlighted shops in the newspaper and work my way through calling each to find out their pricing. In between helping customers, I've managed to set up three appointments to see which building is the best option for what I need.

The bakery phone rings as I finish helping a customer. I wipe my icing covered hands on my apron and pick up the phone with a chipper voice. "Johnson's Jellies, Jams, & Joyful Desserts."

"Andi?" a vaguely familiar voice asks.

"Yes, this is she." I place the phone between my shoulder and ear and grab paper towels to Windex the bakery case. "How can I help you?"

"This is Nana," she says, her smoky tone now recognizable. "Winchester's grandmother."

A flush creeps up my neck, and the heat at my ears tells me they're surely red with embarrassment. I clear my throat and hope my voice doesn't come out shaky.

"Oh, yes. Hi, Nana." I clamp down on the urge to apologize again that I lied to her and tried to help Win swindle her into retirement. "What can I do for you?"

"Could you stop by the firm today to meet with me?"

Blood pulses beneath my skin, rushing in rapids towards my thumping heart. What could she possibly want me to come there for? You can't be sued for lying to someone about dating their grandson. Right? Or would that be considered conning her? Oh my gosh. Am I a con artist now?

My thoughts veer toward Win. We haven't spoken since I left, and to be honest, I'm still too in my head about everything to message him back. Did our blow-up mess up him becoming a partner? Will he be there? Am I ready to see him?

A drink of water or something to wet my dry mouth would be perfect right now.

"Andi? Are you still there?" Nana asks.

"Yes, I'm here," I squeak out. I take a quick, shallow breath and infuse my voice with more confidence than I currently feel. "I can be there around five. Is everything okay?"

"Everything's fine, sweet pea. Don't you worry." She laughs as if she has no care for my poor nerves.

"Okay," I reply, unsure of just about everything.

"I'll see you then."

I give her a hum of agreement before I slump against the bakery case, staring out at the retro black and white checkered tile. What in the world could Win's Nana want to talk to me about? I look at the shelf housing my gnomes—the reason I even went through with Win's stupid idea—and I realize that I'm not sorry I made the deal. I know I should be, but I'm not. I was able to complete more orders than I would've if I sat around at Grams's house in the snowstorm.

People who have a dream should do darn near anything to achieve it—save for conning an elderly woman—and I determined to make my dreams a reality. Having a passion-filled night with the man who's always had my heart was an added benefit.

Time inches by as I wait for the clock to strike four thirty. Another employee clocks in, and I speed home to shower and change and leave for the firm. Bright sun has melted some of the snow from the storm, turning it to dingy slush. The streets are packed with rush hour traffic, and I curse myself for deciding to blow dry my curly hair just in case I run into Win.

Curiosity got the best of me, and I finally looked at his text messages. With each apology, my heart filled with hope. But there's still the lingering doubt in my mind because *he* walked away. When push came to shove and he needed to fight for us, he left.

He made me feel like I wasn't worth fighting for—like my brother did with my parents.

"Hello." A secretary greets me with a genuine smile once I enter the office. "Do you have an appointment?"

"Yes, with Na—Rita Robinson." I nod sheepishly, feeling completely out of place in the formal environment. Beautiful artwork hangs on dark brown walls, and off to the side there's a wall filled with pictures of all the lawyers. Win's picture is easy to spot in the sea of faces with his warm brown skin and devilishly handsome smile. Nana has a good mix of women and men of all ages on the board, a testament to her getting ready to shift the tide of lawyers into a new generation.

"Right this way." The secretary ushers me toward the lit-up hallway filled with a row of doors. My lungs expand rapidly as we walk, and I wonder if Win's here in one of these rooms, chatting up a new client. We stop in front of an open doorway, and the secretary ushers me inside. I peek around the door, slightly worried there might be cops lurking in the corner, ready to arrest me.

Nana sits at a massive, carved mahogany desk with a breathtaking view of the city behind her. Beneath a wall full of framed newspaper clippings celebrating Robinson & Cosley LLP is a long bookcase adorned with pictures of Nana socializing with the mayor and other various figureheads.

"Come in, Andi," Nana says, typing away on her computer without looking up.

The secretary closes the door behind her, leaving me alone with the Robinson matriarch. Sweat forms on my skin as I trudge toward the black wingback chairs in front of her desk, and the leather makes a loud noise as I nestle into it. I rub the pads of my fingers together, waiting for

Nana to stop typing and tell me why I'm here. I check the time on my watch three times in the span of twenty seconds.

My gaze floats around the trinkets and frames on her desk. Pictures of Win at various ages line the top of her cabinetry and bookcase. There's no doubt the woman loves her grandson. But is her love for him enough to absolve me of my guilt for joining in his deceit?

"Stop thinking so loudly," she says, laughing as she spins her chair toward me. "Everything is fine, Andi."

I guess I should've known she'd see through my fake confidence. She's a lawyer trained to get to the nitty gritty of someone's façade. Why I thought she wouldn't see through the lie Win and I cooked up is an error on my part.

"Sorry." I slide my sweaty palms against my dress pants. I would've felt much more comfortable in my jeans and Gnome hoodie, but seeing as I don't know why I'm here, I felt it best to dress to impress. "I'm just nervous."

"There's nothing to be nervous about." She rounds the desk to sit in the chair opposite me. "I wanted to chat with you about something."

"Okay?" My toes curl in my Converse.

"Winchester told me about your deal." She pauses, and I swear my heart is hooked up to a speaker box and is thumping so loudly the entire firm can hear it. "We did some research and found a few other tenants burned by this sleazy landlord, and they all want to come together to file a suit against him."

Air rushes out of me at her words. This is *not* the conversation I expected to be having with her this afternoon. With the pressure gone, I say, "That's great. Well, not great, but you know what I mean." I laugh, nervously twirling the hem of my shirt. "How can I help?"

"Do you want to join in the suit?" she asks.

"I'd love to." I cross and uncross my legs, struggling to keep eye contact. It's like I'm waiting for her to mention what happened between us, or at least ask me what's going on with her grandson, but she's a picture of poise and grace, undeterred by my fidgeting. "What do you need from me?"

"I just needed to ask if you wanted to be involved. I'll send over the paperwork you'll need to sign to have the firm represent you. Sarah will be handling the case."

"Sarah?" My voice is quiet, unsure. Did I misread Win's texts? I thought his apologies and requests to meet up sounded like we could potentially move forward, but maybe he just wanted to get in front of this, apologizing for giving me hope that my landlord wouldn't get away with screwing me over.

"She's one of our top lawyers."

I slump into the seat, confused at her words. Win told me he'd represent me pro bono. I don't have the money to fight this otherwise. Letting out a heavy sigh, I say, "I don't think I'll be able to afford your firm."

Her eyebrows bunch then smooth out along her dark skin as if she was thrown off by my statement. A smile skirts her face, and she pats my arm. "You don't have to worry about that, sweet pea. It's all taken care of." My gaze bounces around the room, searching for a hidden cameraman ready to jump out at me and say "gotcha." When I don't respond, she adds, "Two doors down you'll find the answer you're searching for."

My thoughts flit between worry and excitement. A desire to walk away from this whole fiasco speeds through my mind, but I push it away. I deserve an answer to my questions, and the man with those answers is so close I can smell his fresh bergamot scent.

"Okay." I rise from the chair. "I appreciate your help with this."

"The pleasure's all mine." Playfully nodding toward the door, she adds, "Now go knock some sense into that grandson of mine."

I hold in my laughter and exit her office, the amusement I felt inside melting the minute I step into the hallway and stare down the door she was talking about. I shuffle on my feet, considering whether I want to have this conversation right now. I'm not sure my brain is ready to formulate the words I need to say to him.

I roll my shoulders back and inflate my lungs with a deep breath, pushing the uncertainty aside. The years I spent spent cycling through anger and yearning with the man behind those doors ends today. Either I walk out of here with a boyfriend and a law firm representing my case, or I leave as a single woman ready to move on.

The door opens before I knock, and my bravado sinks into my stomach. Win stands in front of me clean-shaven, hair faded, in a crisp white oxford with his sleeves rolled up to showcase his toned forearms.

"Dandelion Johnson, what a surprise." His voice is like warm honey dripping down my skin. "Did you miss me?"

I scoff, bringing my gaze back to where he leans against the door jamb, those damn sexy forearms crossed in front of his broad chest. A muscle in my jaw twitches, but I don't give him the satisfaction of knowing I'm unprepared to see him.

"As if, Winchester." I push past him, hoping the few seconds it takes to get to the chairs in front of his desk is enough time to slip back on my confident mask. "I wouldn't waste the brain cells."

He laughs, and I hear the click of the door as it closes. Somewhere in my dirty mind, I imagine he locked the door as well, nefarious thoughts of taking me over his desk swirling around his mind. He perches on the edge, purposefully putting me eye level with his lower half. Staring at his crotch, I can see the outline of the titan I've become intimately familiar with.

"My eyes are up here, Dandi."

"Would you stop calling me that?" I grit out in feign annoyance and ever so slowly look at him.

A slow smile builds "Never."

"Ugh, you're the worst."

"Why haven't you answered my messages?"

I shrug. "You had your chance to say whatever you needed to me at your mom's house, but you left."

His shoulders fall slightly, and he glances toward the ceiling as if he's taking a moment to gather his thoughts. I hear his intake of breath a moment before he crouches down in front of me. "I'm sorry, Andi."

I press my tongue into my cheek and glance off to the side, praying away the tears. "Okay."

Win grasps my chin, securing my attention. "I am sorry. For so much more than just walking away the other day. I'm sorry that I let my shit get in the way of what could've been between us. I'm sorry that I let a decade pass when I could've spent that time showing you how much I love you. How much I've always loved you. I was a dumbass kid, and I'm apparently prone to still being a dumbass adult sometimes."

He lets go of my face, but he still has his grip around my heart. "I've spent too much time trying to make up for a mistake that not only took you from me but made me think I didn't deserve anything good. I should've come to you the moment I got released and got my life back on track."

"Win," I sigh, allowing the anger to slide down my back to the floor. "I don't know that it's enough. You've—we've—made a lot of mistakes."

"I know that, but I need you to know there's nothing I wouldn't do to fix those mistakes and to prove to you that we *are* worth it."

My eyes sting, and I can barely hear anything past the thumping in my ears. I'm not that meek, passive girl who let her parents send her away because of *optics* anymore. I want to believe his words, for him to understand that I won't settle for less.

"I mean it when I say you deserve better." He steals the words from my mind. "I didn't fight for you the first time, and I failed again the other day when I left instead of standing up to your brother and being honest with my grandmother. I was a dick, a weak, selfish man, hoping I could have it all without coming to terms with my own feelings about what I deserve and could offer you."

"I don't want anything from you."

He reaches for me, entwining our fingers. "I know."

"No, I don't think you do." I back up, trying to create space between us. People's opinions are like worms that burrow into our core, festering in the soil of our minds. "You're so stuck on what you can offer me, like I need something you can't provide, but love isn't a transaction. I've never needed anything but *you*."

"But—"

"How can I trust that you won't hurt me again?" My voice is shallow, pained as I reopen the wound. "You've done nothing but show me, a decade ago, and two days ago, that when shit gets rough you're going to bail."

A muscle flutters in his jaw, and his shoulders rise as he inhales a deep breath. "Because I learned my lesson that a life without you isn't a life at all."

"Words. That's all they are, Win. I need actions." I want to believe his pretty promises, but if I give in without making it clear what I will and won't tolerate, then I'm setting myself up for heartbreak. "We're not in some court of law where you can lay out your case and have a jury decide that an apology is enough, that you're—we're—no longer guilty of letting a decade pass because we don't know how to communicate."

"For someone who's made a career out of using his words to convey a message, I'm obviously doing a terrible job." He drops to his knees and squeezes my hands. "And you're right. I've done nothing to prove to you that I won't fuck up again. I should've chased you down after the bonfire. I should've stood up to Solo at my house the other day. I should've shown up at your Grams's or the bakery or hunted you down after you left my mom's house. I shouldn't have let you make it five feet away from me without making it clear that there is not a single person in this world for me but you. I didn't do any of that when I should've, but I know what I am supposed to be doing right now. I should be groveling at your feet for another chance to show you I've changed. I can only promise you that from this day on that I will love you loudly, that I won't care what anyone—your parents included—thinks about me or our relationship, that I won't listen to all the negative thoughts that tell me I shouldn't want more than I've already been blessed with."

"You *should* want more for yourself," I reply, staring down at his glassy eyes. "That's the whole reason we ended up here." I gesture around his office. "The entire reason we made the deal in the first place."

Win fixes his confident stare on me. "I could lose the firm tomorrow, and I wouldn't bat an eye. I don't need any of this." He catches my chin between his fingers and tilts my head so he's staring directly into my soul. "But there is one thing I *absolutely* need."

A few things pop into my mind, none of which are appropriate to be thinking about at this moment. With a shaky voice, I ask, "What could you want that you don't already have?"

"You, Dandelion Johnson." He caresses my cheek, and a floating sensation fills me.

Tension dissipates from my shoulders like the burden of the past has been lifted and I'm able to walk into the future with nothing weighing me down.

"There's nothing I need more in this world than to call you mine. To stop wasting another moment feeling like I don't deserve the happiness you bring me. I need you in my life like I need my next breath."

I try—and fail miserably—to blink away the tears forming in my eyes. A floating sensation takes root in my chest after hearing the exact words that I've waited ten years for.

"You had me at 'still a dumbass.'" I grin, snaking my arms around his neck.

Strong arms swoop me up, knocking the chair over in the process. Win wraps my legs around his waist and sets me on his desk. His lips burn a line from my neck to my mouth, leaving searing heat along my skin with his fevered kisses..

"That smart mouth of yours is going to get you in trouble." He pulls my bottom lip down before he places a soft, yearning kiss to my mouth. I feel the truth of his statement pressed up against my thigh, but it's something over his shoulder that catches my attention.

"No way," I breathe out a laugh.

"Yes, way, Andi. The things I plan on doing to that mouth—" I cut off his statement, pushing against his face and sneaking out of his hold. "Where are you going?"

"No freaking way." I stop in front of the bookcase in the corner of the room. There's a copy of *Torts*, *The Tools of Argument*, and other books on constitutional and criminal law, but it's not the books that have my smile touching my eyes. The two bottom shelves of the bookcase are filled with all different kinds of gnomes. Gnomes I whittled and painted and painstakingly decorated for my grandmother to sell.

"You weren't lying." I turn to him with tears streaking down my face.

His laugh is light as he moves closer to me. "You thought I'd lie about them calling me Sherlock Gnomes?" he asks, eyebrows scrunched tight. "Who would lie about something like that?"

I shrug, wiping away the wetness. "Sounds like something a dumbass would do."

He glares at me, growling playfully before he pulls me to him. "Your work is beautiful." He leans past me with a wide grin and grabs one of the gnomes. "This one is my favorite, because it reminds me of you."

Staring down at the figurine in my hand, I can't help but laugh. Upside-down gnome. Blue hat. Green shirt. Long white beard. Holding a sunflower. The Head Over Heels gnome that has always represented us.

Words sit on my tongue, ready to unleash themselves after years of sitting dormant in the back of my mind. I've loved Winchester Robinson since I tumbled over that damn gnome that started my passion, but I know we need to spend time getting to know each other as we are now. No longer kids filled with too many hormones, but adults that understand forgiveness and communication is the only way a relationship can succeed.

I pick up a gnome decorated as the Grinch, gliding my finger over the green hue, reminding me of my lack of shop. "Who is Sarah?" I ask. "And why aren't you representing everyone in the case?"

Win smiles at me, glancing over the features of my face as if he's seeing them for the first time. "It would be a conflict of interest for a partner to represent his girlfriend's case."

"Girlfriend?" My voice cracks a moment before I realize the other portion of the statement my mind missed. "Partner?"

He takes a handful of my ass and squeezes it—like he owns that too. "Yes, Managing Partner."

I lean into his embrace. "But I just saw Nana in her office working?"

"She's sending out emails to let any current clients know about the change, effective in ten business days."

This turn of events is not what I expected to happen after the fiasco we found ourselves in a few days ago. Things are finally looking up, and I for one, am excited to see what the future has in store for us.

"Congratulations," I squeal, pulling his face toward me and peppering him with kisses.

"Wanna celebrate?" His thumbs dust along my hipbone beneath my shirt as they inch toward my pants button. He arches a brow playfully, and I sink my teeth into my lip at the feel of his fingers on my skin. I glance over my shoulder at the closed door, but he turns my gaze back to him. "It's locked."

Chapter Twenty
Win

One Year Later

It should be illegal to be sweaty when it's ten degrees, yet here I stand outside, covered in a nervous sweat, staring at Andi as she closes up her workshop. After finally expanding into home décor, she's been working non-stop to complete her holiday orders before we go on vacation, and I'm ready to whisk her away for a weekend where it's just us.

Lights flicker off as she nears the doorway, already changed into her dress for dinner with my family and her brother. Solomon took a while to get used to seeing us together—he still cringes every time we kiss around him—but he's finally realized there's no stopping our love. Andi's parents took a lot longer to get on board with our relationship. They still look at me like I'm a felon most days, but I'm determined to convince them they have nothing to worry about. Andi doesn't care what they say or if they accept me, but I want them to know I'm taking care of their daughter.

"Ready?" I ask as Andi locks the door and wraps her long down jacket around her.

"I guess so. Where are we going again?" Her nose pinkens quickly, and a few snowflakes land on her long eyelashes. I pull her under my arm, careful not to let her feel what's inside my pocket.

"To dinner. You know that thing you do in the evening when you're hungry."

She pinches my nipple, and it sends a thrill of arousal straight to my groin. "You're such a smartass."

"A smartass that you love." I usher her into the car where the seats are already warmed, and she relaxes into the seat, letting out something between a groan and a moan. Pinching the bridge of my nose, I pray for patience. We have to make it through dinner before I can have her the way I want.

Inside the car, I can't stop from leaning over the console and capturing her lips. She opens, allowing me full access to ravage her mouth. Her exploring hand lands on my cock, rousing the animal caged behind my zipper begging to be let free, and I barely find the strength to pull back.

"Win" she whines, still rubbing my crotch. She bats long eyelashes encasing toffee brown irises I could get lost in and pouts. "We can be a few minutes late, right?"

The little devil on my shoulder snickers. Andi's touch lights me up like a firecracker, and she's the type to hold it until it explodes. Either I sit through dinner with a raging hard-on, or I let her have mercy on me and put me out of my misery.

"Andi," I growl when she pumps me through my dress pants. The determined look on her face shows me she'd rather see me come undone in my pants like a teenager than release me. As if it's a burden, I playfully sigh and say, "Open that pretty mouth for me."

She sensually bites down on her lip, dancing her fingers up to flick open my button and pull down the zipper, revealing my cock already beaded with precum. I'm ready to combust just from her looking at my cock.

"Don't fuck up my hair, Winchester."

I laugh loudly, unsurprised by her candor. She glares at me the entire time she lowers to my cock as if I'm going to forget and touch her curls.

From the moment her breath coasts along the sensitive dome I'm ready to blow, but I clench down on every muscle in my body and will them to stay put. Her tongue darts out, tasting the cum gathered there, and my stomach tightens with restraint.

"Andi, if you don't put my dick in your mouth right now, I'm gonna cum all over your pretty little—"

Warmth encases my dick as she swallows me down, stopping me mid-sentence. Her cheeks hollow out as she comes back up, swirling her tongue around my sensitive tip. I try to think of anything but how good this feels, how simply the thought of being inside her in any way can turn me to mush. In the back of my mind, I know we're sitting in a car in a public parking lot. It's empty, but that just means it'll be even more apparent why we haven't moved yet.

I nearly tell Andi to stop, that we can finish this later, but then she grips me around the base and pumps in time with her mouth. My balls draw up at her slurping and sucking, and euphoria explodes at the base of my spine, barreling straight for my groin.

"I'm coming," I barely rasp out before the sensation hits. She continues sucking and stroking me through my release, and with a pop she sits up, smiling widely at me. "I love you," I say, pulling her to me for a bruising kiss. "Now let's get to dinner so I can repay the favor."

Her smile is devilish. "I'm not hungry anymore."

I struggle to get my pants in order. "You are—"

"Beautiful, amazing, the best cock sucker in the world—"

"The love of my life," I reply, grabbing her hand. "You are everything."

Her face lights up, cheeks pink from exertion. "I love you too, Win. Now let's go pretend like we're not late because I was gobbling down your cock."

I cough out a laugh and get on the road as Andi touches up her red lipstick, her mark still a brand on my skin. Everyone is waiting for us at the restaurant, but I wish I could forgo all the pomp and circus and just take Andi back to our apartment. Since her new workshop is in Boston, we decided to move in together. Our lives are already so entwined that what comes next just feels...natural.

"There they are." Nana whoops as we arrive at the table. "Took ya long enough."

"Hi, sweetie," my mom says, wrapping Andi in a hug before turning to me and whispering, "You ready for this?"

I smile at her and nod. "I was ready ten years ago."

Solomon claps me on the back and draws me in for a hug. "Hey *brother*," he says, emphasizing the word. I asked him for his blessing before I asked her father, knowing that it was her relationship with Solomon that she cared about. Had Solo said no I would have fought him—and won this time—for his blessing.

"I'm starving," Nana says, opening her menu. "Sit down so we can order."

We all laugh at her grouchiness. I pull out the chair for Andi and kiss her once she's seated. The waiter comes back and takes our order, and the entire time we're eating, sweat forms beneath my clothes. I don't tend to get nervous—being a lawyer helped me mitigate any fear of public speaking years ago—but I want everything to be perfect for this woman who gave me a second chance.

After the waiter clears the dinner plates and refills our wine glasses, across the table Solo winks at me. "The weather man said a big storm is rolling in this weekend."

Knowing this is a cue to get my ass ready, I wrap my arm around Andi and slide my hand into my pocket, turning the wood over to soothe my nerves.

"I remember what happened during the last snowstorm," Nana chimes in, playfully glaring at me and Andi across the table.

Andi coughs, nearly spilling the wine in her glass. I pat her back, then reach for her hand, bringing it to my lips for a kiss. "I got the love of my life back."

She blinks up at me through glassy eyes. "You also grabbed my boob after we were nearly pancaked on the road by a truck."

The entire table chuckles at her comment. Leave it to Andi to take what I hope to be a memorable, romantic moment and turn it into a dirty comment. Swiping a loose curl behind her ear, I say, "A lot has changed since that storm." She leans into my touch, and I'm terrified she can feel my thumping pulse. "You sued your sleazy landlord, found a new workshop, expanded your Etsy store, and we moved in together."

"Don't forget Robinson & Cosley's has become one of the go-to law firms under your leadership," she replies, knocking her shoulder into mine. Mom and Nana coo at our little lovefest while Solo mimics barfing. Figuring it's time to get this show on the road, I scoot my chair back and grab Andi's left hand.

"I made something for you," I say, placing the tiny figure into her palm.

Her face lights up as she traces her finger over the wood, marveling at every curve and dip I secretly whittled and painted while she was hard at work completing orders. It took me months—and a shit ton of splinters—before I could even whittle out any semblance of a gnome. It's not perfect, but her wide grin shows me she loves it.

"Holy shit!" Andi's squeal draws the attention of neighboring tables as she stares at the gnome dressed as a carpenter, complete with a tiny hammer and an engagement ring. "When? How?"

She asks the questions, but she's not paying attention to anything but the gnome. I take her distraction as an opportunity to grab Nana's ring from the notch in the gnome and drop down on one knee.

"Dandelion Johnson." I pause, taking a moment to bask in her gaze. I'm well aware the entire restaurant's eyes are on us, waiting with bated breath to watch this unfold, but all I see is my woman. "I never thought I'd be able to call you mine again, to be the one who gets to wake up next to you, to watch you achieve every dream, and to celebrate with you."

She blinks, and a tear drops from her dark eyelashes. I kiss her fingertips and continue before I lose my nerve.

"I spent too many years wishing I could reverse time and steal back the moments we lost to our own stupidity. I know now that we both had to work through some stuff before we could become the people we needed to be for each other. Even through all that time apart, there's something I realized."

Tears streak down her pink cheeks, and I swipe them away with my thumb. She sniffles through a smile. "What did you realize?"

"There's gnome one like you." She lets out a belly laugh at my pun, and there's a collective sigh from those around us as if we're in a Hallmark movie. "Will you make me the happiest man in the world and become my wife?"

Wetness drips onto my fingers, and it takes a moment to realize I'm crying. Staring up at the love of my life, the woman who saw past my façade, I wait to hear her answer. She nods, no words coming from her lips.

"I need words, baby girl."

She lunges forward, nearly knocking me to the ground as she kisses me breathless. "Yes, a million times yes!"

I swoop her up into my arms, placing her on her feet and sliding the family heirloom onto her finger. She stares down at the marquise diamond set in a twisted white gold band, the perfect fit for her slender fingers. After sharing dessert and congratulations with our family and the other patrons that stop by to swoon over her ring and the proposal, we leave the restaurant.

Twinkling multi-colored lights are wrapped around the garland hanging from the lampposts, and the soft crooning tone of Nat King Cole singing about roasted chestnuts floats in the air, playing from the outdoor speakers of a department store across the street. We walk hand in hand, snow crunching beneath our boots and our noses pink with the chill.

"I can't believe it," Andi says as we approach the car.

I open the door for her, thankful for the remote start that already has heat wafting toward us. "Believe what?"

"That I get to spend the rest of my life with you." She stands on tiptoes and kisses me softly, languidly, as snowflakes fall from the sky. I sigh into her, chasing her lips as she releases her hold on me. "Are you gonna tell me where we're going on our weekend vacation?" she asks, sliding into the seat.

"How does the Bahamas sound?" I close the door before she has a chance to respond, giving her a moment to squeal loudly as I run around to the other side. She's been talking about going to the Caribbean since last year, and now that the firm is running smoothly, I feel like I can take time off. And there's no better way to celebrate the woman of my dreams saying yes to spending our lives together.

"Win!" she yells once I'm in the car. Her jaw is slack in shock, but there's a slight turn up at the corners where she's fighting a smile. "The Bahamas?"

"You know me." I shrug with a mischievous smile.

"Don't do it." She giggles, covering her face. "I can't handle anymore puns!"

"Go big or go gnome."

Acknowledgements

There are no words meaningful enough to thank everyone who helped bring this book to fruition.

This is the second book I've published but the first one I've written since my writing career took a tumble down the drain. After my agent and I split, I went through a spell where I *couldn't* write anything. I didn't have the words, and for someone who chose a career as an author that was a big problem. My inspiration was gone. It took me over a year to produce something new, but I got there. While I have other full-length novels, this novella is my baby. The book reminded me that I STILL have those words in me! It was a labor of love trying to fit whole character arcs and an entire plot into 50k or less, but I did it! And I hope you enjoyed it!

Now, to thank some very special people!

First, to God for blessing me with a never-ending well of stories to write.

Second, to my amazing husband who supports and encourages me daily to chase this dream!

Yaya. Did you ever imagine that ceramic gnome we painted all those years ago would spark an obsession with gnomes, and eventually a book idea? I know our spring gnomes broke, but we'll always have this book! Thank you for always listening to my crazy rambling about stories, and for your never-ending encouragement. Also, do you think if I mention

Dutch Bros. in every book that they'll eventually give you an endless supply of Double Chocolate Mocha Freezes with a green straw? I love you, Citag.

Michelle. Mich. My sister. These people don't know it, but they would've been reading an entirely different book if I didn't have you in my life. Honestly, they should all be sending you flowers for everything you helped me dig out of this book, all the foliage you helped me cut down so the story could shine. I'm forever grateful to have you in my life. I love you! P.S. #LOAMY.

Kelly. My co-host for the #ThrillsandChills chat and another writing sister. Have I told you lately how amazing you are? Thank you for your constant encouragement and support of my writing. You're my hype woman and one of my absolute best friends!

My Twisted Sisters. I'm writing this before we go on our writing retreat so if you kill me they will know it was one of you. I'm kidding! Thank you for always being willing to read my romance stories even though we started as a suspense group! Our monthly chats have kept me encouraged and motivated to continue writing when it felt like the words were so far away. Y'all are my cheerleaders, and I cannot wait to hype up your books!

Marysa. My ride or die. It's been about three years now that we've been friends, and I know you're someone I'll be friends with for many years to come. Your early read and feedback were essential to Win's character arc. We love a sad boi who knows he needs to grovel.

I was blessed to have a ton of friends who read multiple versions of this book, and even though I'm sure I'll forget to name a few, I'm at least going to try- Maritza, Farrah, Scarlette, Elizabeth, TT Lex, Bethany, Melissa, and so many more. Thank you.

And to my three reasons for never giving up, my babies. You kiddos show me that life is worth living, that every day brings something new, and that no matter how dirty I think something is, you can make it dirtier. Thank you for always being ready with a hug and a kiss for Mommy. I love you.

Want to read more by Tobie Carter?

THE WORDPLAY SERIES

The Bottom Line

To connect with Tobie:

www.TobieCarter.com
X- @Tobiecarter6190
Instagram- @Tobiecarter.writer
TikTok- @AuthorTobieCarter
Threads- @Tobiecarter.writer

About the author

Tobie Carter is a fiction writer of contemporary romance stories that speak to the reader's heart and leave them with a story that lingers long after finishing. Her stories are fast-paced, angsty, high heat, and feature relatable characters who refuse to settle for less than they deserve. She lives in Central Texas with her husband and three young children.